A ROOM ON THE HILL

ALSO BY GARTH ST. OMER

"Syrop" in *Introduction Two: Stories by New Writers*
Shades of Grey
Nor Any Country
J-, Black Bam and the Masqueraders

A ROOM ON THE HILL

GARTH ST. OMER

INTRODUCTION BY JEREMY POYNTING

PEEPAL TREE

First published by Faber and Faber
in Great Britain in 1968
This new edition published in 2012 by
Peepal Tree Press Ltd
17 King's Avenue
Leeds LS6 1QS
England

ISBN13: 978 1 84523 093 7

Supported by
ARTS COUNCIL
ENGLAND

INTRODUCTION

JEREMY POYNTING

Between 1968 and 1972, Garth St Omer published four books, of which *A Room on the Hill* was the first. Few questioned his ability as a writer. What was at issue was how his fiction related to the project of decolonisation. Gordon Rohlehr's influential essay, "Small Island Blues", is double-edged: it admires St Omer's skills but regrets the perceived pessimism and reluctance to portray characters engaged in anti-colonial revolt.[1] Kamau Brathwaite saw St Omer's work as "negative", part of an existential trend of negativism that connected him to V.S. Naipaul, the Walcott of *The Gulf* (1969), and Orlando Patterson's *An Absence of Ruins* (1967).[2] Peter Dunwoodie wrote of "the utter despondency, the seemingly banal void with which Garth St Omer concludes *J—, Black Bam and the Masqueraders* and, to a large extent, the quartet of which it is more the nadir than the climax".[3] This is par for several other articles.[4] No doubt some contemporary disapproval was also connected to the fact that St Omer wrote about the relatively privileged mulatto middle class in an era when the authenticity of the Caribbean novel was located in its "peasant" credentials.

It is possible, too, that some of the contemporary responses from critics elsewhere in the Caribbean were based on having little notion of what the St Lucia of the 1950s was actually like, and misread realism for negativism.[5] Here Patricia Ismond's (herself St Lucian) generally balanced reading of St Omer's fiction, which puts it into the context of contemporary St Lucian society, is undoubtedly helpful in that it locates the perceived pathology in that society rather than in the author himself.[6]

So what are we dealing with here? A writer who was perceived as being on the wrong side in the contemporary culture wars, a writer who had good reasons for scepticism over the fervour for national independence, or a writer whose pessimism did indeed

5

lead to an artistic and ideological dead end? Retrospective perspectives help us to see how St Omer may have been misread, though they do not in themselves justify why we should read his fiction today. Indeed, one fairly recent survey implies that the neglect of St Omer's work may be due in part to its being bypassed by history – that the late colonial St Lucia he writes about no longer exists[7] – but then neither does Dickensian London. Which, of course, suggests that if *A Room on the Hill* is worth revisiting, it has to be on the basis of its persistent ability to engage us with its vision, with the quality of its writing, its formal shaping, and its insights into people and their interactions.

Room certainly offers a devastating critique of the rootlessness and individualistic selfishness of the St Lucian mulatto elite, of the absolutes of class division, the hypocrisy of the institutional church, and the incestuous suffocations of small island life. In this respect, it connects to other novels of the period, such as Sam Selvon's *I Hear Thunder* (1963), Orlando Patterson's *An Absence of Ruins* (1967) or Andrew Salkey's *The Late Emancipation of Jerry Stover* (1968), but this is not all that *Room* is about. It is the story of a man who has come to life, but is then confronted by the terror that he is about to succumb to somnambulism again. It is also the story of a woman who, unknown to the man – and unnoticed (why?) in the critical commentaries – manifests a Sisyphean courage in revolt that the protagonist desires but does not achieve. It is about the inescapability of death and the challenge to lead an authentic life in times when the consoling certainties of faith are breaking up and the borrowed routines of colonial life have become unendurable. These are historic *and* perennial concerns.

The contemporary response I find most enlightening, though sadly it is brief and unelaborated, is that by Cliff Lashley.[8] Lashley was unquestionably on the side of Kamau Brathwaite's cultural "gorillas" in the nativist, decolonising project, but what he has to say attests to the liberating truth-telling in St Omer's fiction: "St Omer led me unfalteringly to the quicksand edge of my typical life history and left me to my own devices... St Omer is not a prescriptive writer: he is an enabling writer, giving me my life in such a way as I am better able to live it..."[9] This introduction seeks to elaborate the hints embedded in the terms "not... prescriptive" and "enabling" that are at the heart both of what St Omer achieves and why he has sometimes been misconceived.

Form, Implicitness and the Dialogic

In *Room*, form is no mere technical accomplishment, but is oriented to a vision that is dialogic, and to an aesthetic that, contrary to surface appearances, is deeply West Indian in focus. Its narrative begins and ends with the situation of John Lestrade, a civil servant who has been planning to leave the island for higher education in Canada, but who, following the deaths of his best friend, Stephen, and of his mother, has withdrawn to a barrack house on the hill, in a state of suspended animation. Explicitly, the novel is divided into just two parts – before and after Lestrade's friend Harold's return – but in terms of the novel's musical flow, its patterns of parallelisms, its movements between events in the "present" and memories of the past, its deepening cycles of revelation and its dialogic creation of contrary viewpoints, it helps to see it instead as having a four-part structure with a coda.

The first part (chapters 1 to 5) carries us from John Lestrade's meeting with Miss Amelie in the church-yard, his walk home to the barrack room on the hill, mulling over memories of his mother's and Stephen's deaths and meetings with Miriam and Anne-Marie, the former partners of, respectively, his friends Stephen and Derek. Later Lestrade sets off to visit his friend, the old ex-priest, but meets Anne-Marie on the way, who reminds him about Harold's welcome-home party.

The second part (chapters 6 to 9) again focuses on Lestrade, taking us from the day after Harold's homecoming party (and his revelation of the contents of Stephen's letter) to his birthday party six months later, with a similar pattern of Lestrade's meetings (with Anne-Marie and Miriam at the club and his father's visit) and memories (the incident with Chou Macaque,[10] the adolescent fight with his father). In the present, we see Lestrade struggling between a quasi-suicidal dissoluteness and a hesitant awakening to consciousness. At Harold's birthday party, there is a significant switch of focus from Lestrade to Anne-Marie and the artist, Dennys.

The third movement (chapters 10 and 11), which begins with a beach party for Derek's return, is seen entirely through Anne-

Marie's eyes, and represents a powerful parallel and critique of the patterns of the first two movements focused on Lestrade. This movement ends with what we discover will be Anne-Marie's accidental death.

The fourth movement (chapter 12), a tour-de-force of narrative construction, is focused around Anne-Marie's funeral and brings together four strands of literal and symbolic movement: Dennys' Sisyphean trek from the hospital to join the funeral; Harold's and Derek's collision with the forces of Catholic obscurantism (the refusal to allow a burial service, first, second or even third class); the funeral cortege itself; and the children's unruly procession behind Old Alphonse, which switches to following the funeral when they see Dennys perched on the back of the hearse. The confluence of these movements is brilliantly done (pp. 145-147).

The last chapter (13) is by way of a coda, and deals with the crisis of consciousness that Lestrade has been returned to.

A Room on the Hill is not a perfect novel – there are lapses into rather obvious metaphor (the drowning rats in the cages in the sea) and an awkward deus ex machina in the appearance and sudden death of the Martiniquan woman (in a novel where accidental death plays perhaps too strategic a role) – but how many Caribbean novels manage to say so much in so little space? Developing writers could learn much from close attention to the way St Omer pays his readers the courtesy of assuming that they will read in an active hypothesis-creating and questioning mode – not least in "reading" implicit cues about the social and cultural location of characters – rather than as passive consumers of authorial confidences and explanations.

Just in the first few paragraphs, without any commentary, we are given the class/race location of the speakers, Lestrade's ambivalence about his faith, the back story of his mother's death, several mysteries (What are people saying? Who is Stephen and why no grave?), the embedding of the spiritual in the commercial and the theme of the unknowability of others ("he felt like a spy" (p. 30). What St Omer achieves throughout the novel is a fictive referentiality with few of the usual translations, paraphrases and explicitly explanatory sentences that interrupt the flow of many Caribbean literary texts for the benefit of their UK, or more latterly North American markets.[11] It's a style of telling that is also wholly appropriate for a small island narrative where people share a core of reference. This may seem a small issue, but it is a pointer to St Omer's commitment to a Caribbean vision – however uncomfortable.

Concerning another of the pleasures of the text – the recognition of fruitful literary allusion – it's worth elaborating upon Gordon Rohlehr's perception that St Omer has learnt from Joyce's objective in *Dubliners* of "scrupulous meanness".[12] *A Portrait of the Artist* and the early chapters of *Ulysses* are other significant intertexts, and one can take from them not only the obvious connections, but a hint at what St Omer saw himself aiming at: a fiction that was simultaneously rooted in nation and bent on escaping from the nationalistic. There are the themes of a mutually destructive mother/son relationship, clerical repression and internal exile, and there is also a creative refashioning of the metaphor of the cloak, Stephen Dedalus's ubiquitously iconic image. McCann's charge in *A Portrait of the Artist*, "– Dedalus, you're an antisocial being, wrapped up in yourself"[13], is no less pertinent to Lestrade. We see him first with the "dark of the night [...] comfortable about his shoulders" (p. 46), are told that "His [spiritual restlessness] he had been able to cover with the cloak of his several affairs" (p. 59), and of "the friendships which he had used like cloaks" (p. 90). Such images should alert us to see how St Omer uses the figurative to create dialogue with the novel's literal realism. This is evident in the reversal of the image in the case of Anne-Marie, when she sheds the cloak of legitimacy (the school uniform) bought by her father's social influence:

> She tore her uniform away from her body. Its feel on her skin was abhorrent. Its elegance was at once symbol of her father's duplicity and the hypocrisy of an entire existence. (p.128)

And the metaphor is continued in the description of the commitment she makes to her personal decolonisation:

> But the disintegration of the fabric of their personal relationship was the prelude to the greater disintegration, more gradual, of the entire fabric of her previous existence. Out of this disintegration [...] her new life developed and expanded,

achieving a new diversity, social and moral, that overran the former plot lines of its exclusiveness. (p. 128)

It is possible that the economies of compression St Omer achieves here has led to readings which fail to see that the voice of his "main" character is by no means the most privileged, or which don't notice how he quite frequently makes subtle but clear shifts between the free indirect presentation of a character's thoughts and the narrator's voice. Even Patricia Ismond's insightful piece becomes fixed around the idea of a St Omer "persona" who is male, socially disengaged and self-cripplingly introspective, and this comes to stand for the world-view of the novels, not as an acute analysis of a particular kind of failure.

Existential Themes and Historical Realism

There has been a tendency to see St Omer's evident familiarity with the literary movement of European existentialism as something of an excrescence in his fiction.[14] Some of the contemporary difficulty may have been to do with the feeling that existentialism was a European fad, and that the introspection it encouraged was a middle-class luxury and diversion from a proper focus on the folk. With the luxury of hindsight, the work of African American scholars, such as Lewis R. Gordon, on the existentialism of Fanon and the African diaspora[15] – which came some decades later – should remind us that there is nothing inherently un-Black or un-Caribbean in asking philosophical questions about the nature of existence. Still, accepting this doesn't tell us how well St Omer integrates the philosophical and the fictional in his writing. I'd argue that as a scrupulous realist and historically acute novelist, St Omer locates his exploration of existential themes effectively, in the particular class, gender, race and institutional frameworks of the time of the novel's setting. Stephen's and Lestrade's regular walks through the cemetery are not just a memento mori, but a lesson in race and class, "from the paupers' end where the graves were unmarked mounds of sand [...] past the concrete and occasionally marble tombs of the very rich..." (p. 58). And death as the dominant reality of his life challenges Lestrade to arrive at a philosophy of existence, and this takes the narrative in a trajectory from the psychology of a particular character's responses to his experiences to his attempt to make philosophical sense of them.

Lestrade's starting point is his shallow, small-island perception that here all are trapped like automatons, whilst real life happens elsewhere:

> There was a key in his back as there were keys in the backs of all the inhabitants of the island. And those keys, it was the island itself that manipulated them. (p. 57)

Deeper questioning begins with his doubts that he shares Stephen's religious consolations, doubts that become acute after his friend's drowning, and the guilt his inaction spurs in him. These thoughts leave him feeling trapped in a state of death-in-life that is altogether more painful than being an automaton. His mother's death further challenges his belief in transcendental consolation, and when he meets Miss Amelie, he cannot evade the contradictions he sees in hers and his mother's lives:

> Yet for her, as it had been for his mother, to die surely was the ultimate Salvation. [...] Death was the ship she would sail on. And death was precisely what she, as his mother had done on her sick bed for three years, would fight against all her life. (p. 39)

The passage to deeper reflection takes Lestrade through quasi-suicidal impulses when he "wanted to consume himself in one continual, inebriated effort until he dropped, from exhaustion, into a state which [...] would be analogous to the state of death" (p. 96). It is during his round of haunting the drinking clubs that he has another brush with death (that of the young Martiniquan woman, Agnita), which reinforces his sense of death's absoluteness and drives him towards a philosophy of existence. It is perhaps an artistic flaw that this realisation is expressed in narrative commentary, not narrative action, and one that pays a rather too direct a homage to Camus, though Lestrade's conclusion – that suicide could be seen as an act of revolt – is not Camus':[16]

> He knew now what made gods possible. And religion too. They gave the lie to reality and carried man safely across the inexplicable. They turned him into a child again, made him irrespon-

11

sible, freed him from the load of himself. And of others. And sitting alone in the dark, it occurred to him that if Stephen despaired, it was because he lost confidence in his God and, losing it, was confronted with the ultimate, final authority for the first time – himself. The revelation of his God, incarnate, but made man now only in himself, might have been too much for him to bear. And his suicide, far from being an act of despair, might have been one of revolt. (p. 105)

But how, then, to lead a life? At first Lestrade's response is stoic evasion. Even though his meeting with Agnita has touched him more than he can believe possible, he decides "He would feel neither regret nor sorrow for the dead girl" (p. 85). But in the brief encounter, Lestrade has seen more than just the possibility of connection; he glimpses something of the actual fluidity of the person and the way a life might be remade in a world where man is his own and only god. The perception begins in drunken play-acting, and the gross lie about the woman he loved dying in childbirth, but the lie makes him feel alive as he senses that despite the pretence, some "rancidity" has been let out. The phrase St Omer uses ("For some time while they walked he continued to *fabricate* his allegory" [my italics]) hints at a fictive kind of truth that begins in the ambivalence of the meanings of "fabricate" – to make/to lie – and in the sense that allegories are truth-seeking. The persona in this instance is inauthentic, but the process hints at the possibility that the self can be remade.

Always, though it is death that Lestrade comes back to (the final room on the hill), spending "long hours among the English dead in the small military cemetery" (p. 108). Here, and in his relationship with the old ex-priest, Lestrade arrives at a moment of Wordsworthian peace in withdrawal ("Alone, he walked, read and thought" (p. 108)), but it is a state of equilibrium destined to be upset by Anne-Marie's death, which returns Lestrade almost, but not quite, to where he has been before.

Collectivity and Connection
Commentary on St Omer's fiction has tended to focus exclusively on his portrayals of solitary, solipsistic individuals and to assume this represents an authorial view on the impossibility of

community and collective endeavour. *A Room on the Hill* does convey powerfully the prevalence of selfish individualism amongst the middle-class milieu of its main characters, but I'd argue that there is a counter-discourse in the novel that places human connection at the heart of what makes life desirable, and also offers us glimpses of not only its necessity but its possibility.

It is true that Lestrade indulges in a feast of solipsistic introspection and arrives at the conclusion that not only amongst his circle, but historically: "Expediency, utility and, ultimately, self-interest, national or individual, was the only criterion" (p. 108), but are Lestrade's conclusions St Omer's? It is certainly true that the novel portrays very acutely the difficulties of connecting to and knowing others. But it is the character's isolation that lies behind his rages, the fact that there is no true collectivity he can engage with, just an atomised group of individuals competing for limited prizes. Lestrade's mutually damaging relationships with his mother and father lead him to feel, "It's a pity we should so be able to affect other people's lives". That learnt wariness is undoubtedly one of the factors (along with his sexism) that kills his relationship with Rose, though there is a deliberate ambiguity between what is particular to Lestrade's limited perceptions, and the suggestion that these limitations are intrinsic to all human contact:

> The old wall had sprung up between them. [...] It was the wall of human selfishness and misunderstanding, of imperfectly explained and imperfectly understood motives and, though they might have been able to get over it singly, they could never, together, scramble over its ugly top. (p. 52)

The one person with whom Lestrade connects is the old Australian ex-priest. If the old man is clichéd in quoting John Donne's "No man is an island", his perception that connection has to be worked at is part of the novel's counter-discourse of possibility. Also countering the novel's apparent pessimism is that, out of Lestrade's sight, there is Dennys' and Anne-Marie's relationship and, beyond his circle, the sociability of the fishermen who rescue Dennys. Above all, there is the brief connection that Lestrade makes, beyond the boundaries of class, with Agnita, the Martiniquan woman, who "had come out of her own little life, whatever it had been, to meet him. And she had left her touch even more than Stephen or his mother had done. And she, a complete stranger" (p. 104). The old ex-priest's insistence, that sociability is a duty not a right, is perhaps the novel's challenge.

Remaking the Colonial World

It should be evident that I think there has been undue eagerness to see St Omer's fiction as negative, to charge it with a failure to address ways out of the colonial impasse. On the contrary, I think that *A Room on the Hill* explores both the difficulty and the necessity of finding a way out of colonialism and the kind of anti-colonialism that is conceptually fixed in static images of the past, that at best rhetorically reverses, at worst cynically inherits, colonialism's structures and values, but does not remake them. At a metaphorical level, at least, the novel connects to the kinds of arguments Wilson Harris makes in several of the essays in *Tradition, the Writer and Society* (1967).

More prosaically, the novel contrasts the need for critical rationality (needed because it offers the potential for change), with the trap of emotional cycles of resentment and recrimination. For instance, Lestrade's attempts at self-understanding are undermined by the continuing power of his wounded emotional responses to his parents. As the narrator comments (in one of those subtle movements between a free indirect passage that reflects Lestrade's consciousness and an external, quietly judging, narrative voice):

> There were so many things about his mother and his father he would have liked to know. There was so much to understand. And it had been so easy not to understand and, not understanding, take up set positions. (p. 83)

And just so we don't miss the point, there's the comment made by Johan, the Polish Jew, at Harold's party, (who sounds surprisingly lucid after a long night of drinking): "'What we need', Johan said, 'is intelligence and understanding'" (p. 113).

Stasis is also the consequence of accepting the past as given. We see Lestrade and his friends talking and talking, but rarely setting out to understand the frameworks of race, gender and class and the very specific nature of the island's external/colonial Catholicism that trap them in dependency. They are, for instance, incurious about the culture of the black majority, represented only in de Beaulieu's dusty antiquarian folklorism; and it is significantly from an outsider that Lestrade learns anything about how he fits into his history: "The Abolition of Slavery had always been for him, up to that time, a phrase only. It was the old man who made him feel that he was a part of that phrase" (p. 93) The same lack of historical awareness is noted in D'aubain's action in buying his daughter's freedom from the mark of illegitimacy (p. 126).

But protest against colonialism on its own is not enough, though Lestrade's emotional rejection of the goals of professional status and money, and his self-contemptuous, Naipaulian critique of the colonial mind ("A race of imitators. […] The most inept, too […]Bloody clowns. All of us" (p. 97)) nevertheless offer the spark of possibility towards his becoming something else. His rage reaches towards authenticity – as the narrative voice wants to persuade us:

> "Fuck every fucking thing," he repeated, mumbling the words. "Why the hell should I care?"
>
> He said it like someone who cares and, caring, pretends he does not. (p. 98)

And the drive to change, when it comes, is portrayed as corporeal as well as cerebral. Lestrade feels "vague stirrings of the spirit [that] made his life uncomfortable. They were like the itch on his body of a skin he was in the process of discarding" (p. 92), an image that connects to Anne-Marie's action in decisively rejecting her colonial condition.

The fact that Lestrade cannot articulate an alternative to the colonial mindset which he rejects is a matter of realism and truth to character, but I think we are also meant to see that what is important is his awareness that a new life cannot be ready-made out of the scraps of the colonial past. The dangers of being condemned to repeat that past are brilliantly caught in passage describing his consciousness of coming to the edge of a new life, in the metaphorical switches that move progressively backwards in time from pathology, via archaeology to paleontology – from the recently dead to the world before human history:

> [H]e had exhumed corpses of his old self; probing them with the
> scalpel of his new awareness, lifting his motives delicately out of
> their integuments to look at them. He had felt very very fragile
> and absolutely dangerous. He had been like an archaeologist
> collecting fossils to recreate a future only. (p. 46)

At first the idea of probing the old self sounds worthwhile, except
that the surgeon pathologist in the metaphor seems to imagine he
is investigating living tissue (why else would he feel dangerous?),
a point made clear by the second misapprehension: the archaeologist who has confused his role with the paleontologist's. By
contrast, the route out of stasis is conveyed in images of uncer-
tainty, inchoateness, but also extensive potential: "The whole sea
of possibility stretched before him and the wind of his urge filled
him and pushed him blindly" (p. 96). And, the sense of a journey
scarcely begun is returned to in the comparison between Lestrade
and the Polish Jew at Harold's party – a statement of recognition
but also of warning against premature closure, against making
confident assertions about what constitutes a West Indian/Carib-
bean identity:

> They had something in common: an identity to establish, a
> position to assert, a phantom to flesh. They were two beings in
> an alien world: one, traditional, recognised, persecuted; the
> other, *young, emergent, as yet unrecognisable to itself or others*. One
> was lost because too observed. The other because too unob-
> served. (p. 113) [my italics]

These are images that arise in the authorial voice, and there is a gap
between them and the most positive and self-perceptive statement
that Lestrade is shown to make: he says he is waiting for change,
though he does not know how it will come or what it will be. The
novel recognises both the perils and discomforts of this position
("the paralysis [that] made any reconstruction in the future too
daring for him to contemplate" (p. 47)) but, through the voice of
the old ex-priest, counsels the necessity for patience. When Lestrade
confesses to feeling like "a very small piece of wood drifting on a
wide sea", the old man tells him to drift: "Somewhere at the end of
your drifting, sometime, there will be land" (p. 92).

This sense of there being something to be sought beyond the given is delicately conveyed in the contrasting images of restriction and extension when Lestrade visits the club by the sea:

> The lights of the club came on, suddenly, shutting out all that was outside their radius. The sea was now only the sound of itself breaking and running up the sand. Gradually his eyes became accustomed again and he could see the white luminous crests of the waves as they broke beyond the area of light, and, in the distance behind them, the flat darkness of the sea. (p. 91)

Lestrade's openness stands against Harold's closure of possibilities. Harold, a lawyer, has come back to the island to make his fortune and establish a position of power through the "new" politics. As Dennys accuses: "You go away and come back qualified […] And all you think of is money, money, money […] and your place in the island's warm social sun, mass-produced in your education, mass-produced in your intentions afterwards; empty, empty, empty" (p. 118). Harold represents those who will inherit post-independence power without in any way dismantling colonial structures. In contrast to Harold, come to claim his place in the sun, Johan, the visiting Polish Jew, tells Lestrade he is:

> … worried about the current talk in the West Indies about Nationalism. He distrusted it. The sickness, he said, would begin with John's politicians and would eat through like a cancer. It would thrive on the ignorance of the electorate, on the disinterring of what had been forgotten and were now insults. And the writers, the ones who were not careful, would speak of evolution and progress, like the politicians. It was a mess, but that was where it would end, as it always did. (p. 113)

One suspects that some of St Omer's contemporary critics read his scepticism about the direction of politics in the region (and I think here that St Omer does use Johan as a proxy) as evidence of his negativity towards the project of decolonisation. I think the novel's metaphorical patterning expresses a desire for genuine sovereignty – the freedom to reconstruct and build more egalitarian and culturally inclusive societies that motivated many in the region – but political realism dictated that the narrative of the novel offers a prescient warning about where nationalist politics was heading in a fair number of post-independence states. We learn that Harold, the coming man, "had already acquired, after only six months, quite a few small estates [...] there hung about him more than a faint smell of dishonesty and the unattractive aura of opportunism and exploitation" (p. 120). This is capped by his "passage into politics [...] another stage in that journey he had mapped out for himself towards ultimate, absolute self-fulfil-ment. And he had begun by writing articles in the island's newspaper that were adverse to Government" (p. 121). It could be objected that St Omer appears to see no alternative to the politics of the brown middle class en route to wealth, but this may well have been an honest response to the absence of any alterna-tive, in St Lucia at least, that genuinely represented the interests of the black majority in the 1950s.[17]

Gendering the Anti-Colonial Revolt

The failure to read *Room* as more than a negative commentary on Caribbean possibilities is nowhere clearer than in the absence of discussion of what it has to say about gender relations. It took a woman writer, Pam Mordecai, talking about gender issues in Caribbean writing in c.1984, to recognise that in *Nor Any Country* (1969), St Omer's third book, he makes "the first honest, decent attempt that I think that a West Indian male sensibility has made to analyse in a rigorous kind of way the whole business of how a man deals with a woman".[18] I'd add that in *Room*, too, the treatment of gender achieves that kind of honest perception, and that it is through the role of Anne-Marie that the novel becomes most clearly dialogic in its tension between possibility and failure.

The novel displays sensitivity to the power of gender and patriarchal attitudes in family relationships, including a Joycean focus on the vexed relationship of mothers and sons in Lestrade's adolescence, a suffocating and resentful dependency replicated in his friend Stephen's relationship with his mother, Teacher Amy. Both of these mother-son relationships suggest the difficulty of achieving responsible manhood when, in the absence of the father, the son feels prematurely bound to mimic a paternal role. This is what lies behind Lestrade's shame/rage that he can't protect his mother from Chou Macaque. A further complication is the Catholic iconography of suffering between the holy mother and martyred son, exemplified by the status Teacher Amy gains when she loses her first son, killed in the 1939-45 war. The other side of this gendered family dynamic is Lestrade's Oedipal rage against the not quite absent father: "He could have killed his father very easily then" (p. 80). Destructive class and gendered expectations of male status are passed on, too, in the D'aubain household, where Anne-Marie's father responds to the wound of public mockery he has suffered at his own father's hands by conducting his sexual relationships only with his servants, impregnating Anne-Marie's mother and then sending the mother away. These are personal tragedies, but Lestrade also acknowledges such behaviour as part of "the precocious sexual aggressiveness that was a tradition of his own island" (p. 48), marked by the sexual predatoriness of the young civil servants "only wanting to accumulate money", who want mistresses but "did not want to marry them". And though Lestrade is portrayed as more gender aware, it does not stop him from behaving in an appallingly sexist way towards the much younger Rose.

It is an undeveloped element in the novel, but it is perhaps significant that the one man who offers a relationship rooted in mutual respect is the old ex-priest who is probably gay, as the unfortunately phrased description of "his effeminacy" suggests.

However, a claim for St Omer's attentive examination of gender in *Room*, and for the novel's dialogic qualities, must rest above all in the role of Anne-Marie. Until the end of the second movement, she is seen as Derek's abandoned fiancée, a peripheral and embarrassing figure to Lestrade's circle, though she is also seen to offer Lestrade direct and honest comfort after his mother's death, and is glimpsed through his gaze, coming towards him "striding like a stallion" (p. 32).

Anne-Marie comes more closely into view at Harold's party, where she is drawn to the embattled artist, Dennys. Here Dennys is the bohemian outsider, engaged in a very unequal quarrel with the assembled ranks of the aspiring middle class, who are berating him for his lack of ambition. She, in contrast, sees a kindred spirit:

> [...] admired his mad, unthinking independence[...] It was possible the painter exaggerated: his talent, his attitude no less

than his speech… Her intelligence told her so. But the kinship she felt for him now was not based on the intelligence. And, in any case, she had been mentally nodding her head in agreement with much of what he had been saying. (p. 119)

If John Lestrade has gone round in circles, never quite reaching a position of clear-sighted revolt, Anne-Marie has steadfastly occupied that position since the day when, as a schoolgirl, she rejected the uniform of false legitimacy. She is the conscious, mature, Camusean rebel who, no less than Lestrade, has seen the absurdity of existence, felt the temptations, but persists with the Sisyphean task. She is no less self-questioning, no less given to probing beneath the surface of things. When she thinks about the sources of her happiness with her former fiancé, Derek, she is shown as perceptively self-aware:

How much of it had been because, refusing to be manipulated, she had perceived an intense emotion in performing actions that would, normally, have given merely pleasure. To love was not rare nor, the popular films notwithstanding, even wonderful. But to love when love was prohibited, to walk when they expected you to fall, to laugh when they waited for you to cry, then that was something else. (p. 131)

But if she has found pleasure in thumbing her nose at racist disapproval of her relationship as a white woman with a black man, compared with Lestrade and Dennys, Anne-Marie's revolt has been an adult one. She has handled – all without self-dramatisation or self-pity – the discovery of her father's hypocrisy and her illegitimacy, Derek's betrayal, and the knowledge of how she is judged in local society. This is not due to any absence of feeling or resignation to suffering. She sits on the beach looking at Derek with his new white wife and family, "feeling acutely the pain of her reminiscence and of his presence" (p. 129). She achieves a detachment that does not deny the reality of the attachment, knows she will always "feel the pain of the past", but will savour the happiness that once existed, like "someone looking at a photograph of the place where, once, he had had a very enjoyable holiday" (p. 130). Her courage is like that of Camus' Sisyphean hero who "at each of those moments when he leaves the heights and gradually sinks towards the lairs of the gods, he is superior to his fate. He is stronger than his Rock";[19] this courage is expressed in her thought: "Well, […] now, an end, not the end" (p. 132). Though she, too, knows the temptations of self-extinction, her response, unlike Stephen's, is to begin the ascent again:

> She felt tired, as after a long swim. Her tiredness was not unpleasant nor unrefreshed. The feeling was like sinking, all breath exhaled, slowly in the warm water. One sometimes felt one should like to sink so pleasantly forever. Then there was the pain in the chest, the need for air and the quick push back to the surface. Always there was the need to be reasonable. Or else. (p. 130)

It is not that St Omer makes a paragon of Anne-Marie (though the reader might wonder if she is rather too much a Lauren Bacallish character from a Howard Hawks' film – but perhaps none the worse for that!). We see that her capacity for energy, pleasure, desire has an edge of desperation, and the rough edges and imperfections of her relationship with Dennys are clearly drawn: its recklessness, its over-familiarity with alcohol, Dennys' macho posturing, the edge of need hinted at in the line: "Whatever he wanted she would give him, when he wanted it and where" (p. 133). And it is perhaps a failure of narrative imagination to have presented Anne-Marie's consciousness so authorially, in contrast to the free indirect representation often used for Lestrade, but even so, she muscles into the narrative in a way that has been strangely missed in most critical commentaries. Even Patricia Ismond's gender-aware reading reduces Anne-Marie to merely a "casualty", "the hedonist, a lone, unlikely figure in St Omer's world".[20] On the contrary, it seems to me that one of the novel's crucial judgements on Lestrade is that he neither recognises nor imagines the inner effort Anne-Marie makes to deal with her much more objectively real reasons for despair. His vision of Anne-Marie is admiring but wholly external: "elegant sensuous and beautiful, going on forever, like a glittering top under the bright lights of all the drawing-rooms of the world" (p. 109), an image which reminds of the constricting light in the club by the sea that prevents Lestrade seeing what is beyond.

The Coda: So where does the novel leave us?

Lestrade is "more alone than he had ever been" after the old ex-priest's departure; after the humiliations of his ambivalent and self-defeating declaration of affection for Miriam; after hearing about the breakdown of his old teacher and seeing in it his own fate. As he did after Stephen's death, he returns to feeling "dead alive, suffocated by the poisonous air of the island he had not been able to get away from" (p. 150). But if he has resumed the automaton's life of drinking, sleeping around, dancing, gossiping in the clubs, he remains alert to the fact that this is an automaton's life. If he is tempted to believe even "in those things he had come to discredit after Stephen had died" (p. 150), he cannot. If he is drawn to envy the complaisance of those who return "failures", Dennys' "beaten acceptance", Harold's "independence", Father Thomas's belief, he knows he cannot lead their lives. If he reflects longingly on childhood, "when he could move easily from day to unthinking day" (p. 151), he knows that this was ignorance, not innocence. He can no longer see death as just an accidental "calamity", but as the central fact of life. He is simultaneously the existential protagonist who has cleared the decks of illusion, and the frail, isolated, unsupported and life-damaged man who wants to be free from the consciousness of life as absurd.

But even if Lestrade is left at a point of despair – a failure, a pessimistic figure with a view of the Caribbean that is backward, with a sense of hopelessness about its future – are we to read St Omer as celebrating this nihilism? I think not. What he does is to undertake a mercilessly honest study of a temperament, of a man who sheds certain illusions but who is still the product of his colonial education, his class and its culture. Moreover, as this introduction has emphasised, Lestrade's is not the only story, and in the other narrative, Anne-Marie's, we see a character who has freed herself from the entrapments of race and class.

If St Omer's honesty was too uncomfortable to be appreciated in 1968, we are in a better position now to acknowledge its virtues. This is not because as readers we are any smarter, but because we can see that the need for ideologically convenient and monolithic ideas about identity has passed, or at least is no longer respectable. We have been taught by the writing of women, gays and lesbians, and the region's ethnic minorities that the fabric of Caribbeanness has to accept all diversities, including those of intellectual reservation. In its uncomfortable art, *A Room on the Hill* deserves our renewed attention and respect.

End Notes

1. "Small Island Blues", *Voices* vol. 2, no. 1 (Sept–Dec 1969), reprinted in *St Lucian Literature and Theatre: An Anthology of Reviews*, eds. John Robert Lee and Kendel Hippolyte (Castries: Cultural Development Foundation, 2006), pp. 15-19.
2. See for instance Kamau Brathwaite, *LX: The Love Axe/l*, vol. 1 (Leeds: Peepal Tree Press, 2012), p. 89, 105.
3. "Images of Self-Awareness in Garth St Omer's *J—, Black Bam and the Masqueraders*", *Caribbean Quarterly*, vol. 29, no. 2 (1983), pp. 30-43.
4. See Gerald Moore, "Garth St Omer", in *Contemporary Novelists*, ed. James Vinson (New York: St Martin's Press, 1972), pp. 1084-1086. Jacqueline Kaye's "Anonymity and Subjectivism in the Novels of Garth St Omer", *Journal of Commonwealth Literature* vol. 10 (1975), pp. 45-52, is an example of criticism that wholly blurs author and characters.
5. It is evident from sources such as Gordon Lewis's *The Growth of the Modern West Indies* (New York: Monthly Review Press, 1968; page references are to the Ian Randle Publishers reprint of 2004) that at a point where Jamaica, Trinidad, Guyana, and to a lesser extent Barbados, had long begun to break free of the colonial cocoon, St Lucia was still firmly wrapped in it. It lacked the progressive middle-class nationalist political leadership and black-led working-class movements that had been creating change elsewhere, for instance in other small islands such as Grenada and St Kitts. It was economically impoverished, grant-aided, controlled directly by the British treasury (Lewis, p. 147). By the 1950s, when *A Room on the Hill* is set, it was only just embarking on the "banana revolution" (now killed by global free-trade capitalism) that brought a measure of rural prosperity. It was, in Lewis's words "semi-feudal", where "the merchants, the large land-owners… the middle class civil servants ruled the inarticulate peasant and or worker with an iron hand" (p. 150). Locking this quasi-feudal economic power in place was the ideology of the Roman Catholic church, almost wholly staffed by white expatriates (mostly from France) who taught obedience, guilt and acceptance of miserable poverty; who tried to discipline the people by having three grades of

funerals (or none, as St Omer alludes to in the case of Anne-Marie) and different school uniforms for the children of the married and "unmarried". There was no politician/historian such as Eric Williams bringing a sharp awareness of the injustices of a past that needed redress; St Lucia's "official" historian was a white priest, Father C. Jesse, whose *Outlines of St Lucia's History* (1970 – it was being reprinted up to 1994) offered an old-fashioned apology for empire. Even as late as 1958, the Catholic hierarchy succeeded in banning Roderick Walcott's play, *The Banjo Man*, from performance.

6. See Patricia Ismond, "The St Lucian Background in Garth St Omer & Derek Walcott", *Caribbean Quarterly*, vol. 28, nos. 1 & 2 (March–June 1982), pp. 32-43.

7. Jane King, "Introduction", *St Lucian Literature and Theatre*, pp. xvi-xvii. The second part of the statement is obviously true. Since St Lucia's belated independence in 1979, it has evidently become a more open society in which the power of the Roman Catholic church and the euro-centric elite has diminished, and the culture of the black majority has been recognised.

8. Lashley was so angered by V.S. Naipaul's provocations at the famous 1971 ACLALS conference at Mona that he allegedly said that Naipaul ought to be shot.

9. "Garth St. Omer: Novelist", *Caribbean Quarterly*, vol. 17, no. 1, (1971), pp. 58-59. Lashley also makes the point that "Before St Omer's work I am unable to find anything in my university study of English literature that is useful in helping me to comprehend… and deepen my experience of the work."

10. The connections with Derek Walcott's contemporary play *Dream on Monkey Mountain* in the naming of Chou Macaque (in *Dream*, the parallel character is called Makak) and John Lestrade (in *Dream*, Makak's opponent is the mulatto Corporal Lestrade) are very likely not so much intertextual references as joint references to the same cultural understandings, but they further illustrate St Omer's economy of implicitness. Grasping the cultural reference makes sense of why Lestrade has felt quite so humiliated as an adolescent when he comes home to find Chou Macaque (monkey man, bongo man) abusing his mother. We are not told the substance of the abuse, but can guess that Chou has been delighting, as a proletarian black man, in pointing out that, for all her pious "brown" respectability, Lestrade's mother is single with an illegitimate child whose "red" (i.e. near white) father is conspicuously absent.

11. Do the editors at Faber deserve some credit here for preserving the novel's implicitness?

12. "Small Island Blues", *St Lucian Literature and Theatre*, p. 16; Joyce's phrase comes from a letter to his publisher in 1906, quoted in Richard Ellmann, *James Joyce* (Oxford: OUP, 1959, 1982), p. 210.

13. *A Portrait of the Artist* (Harmondsworth: Penguin Books, 1963; first published 1916), p. 177.

14. See for instance Jacqueline Kaye's "Anonymity and Subjectivism in the Novels of Garth St Omer". See note 4.

15. See for instance *Fanon and the Crisis of European Man: An Essay on Philosophy and the Human Sciences* (New York: Routledge, 1995) and *Existentia Africana: Understanding Africana Existential Thought* (New York: Routledge, 2000).

16. In *The Myth of Sisyphus* (London: Penguin Books, 2000; first published in the UK in 1955), Camus sets out to examine whether, taking as read that the world is absurd (i.e. irrational in any human sense and godless), suicide is a legitimate response. He concludes that it is not, that living without illusions, with the Sisyphean courage to keep climbing the hill, is the proper response.

17. The St Lucian trade union movement of the 1950s and 60s seems to have been largely a vehicle for aspiring politicians, not really expanding until the 1970s. See Robert J. Alexander, *A History of organised Labor in the English-Speaking West Indies* (Westport, USA: Praeger, 2004).

18. See Daryl Dance, *New World Adams: Conversations with West Indian Writers* (Leeds: Peepal Tree Press, revised ed. 2008), p. 190.

19. *The Myth of Sisyphus*, p. 109.

20. Ismond, "The St Lucian Background", p. 36.

"Only the gulls, hunting the water's edge
Wheel like our lives, seeking something worth pity."

Derek Walcott, "A Careful Passion"

PART ONE

1

Impulsively he left the asphalted road and followed to its top the flight of concrete steps that wound its way up the hill. It was cooler here, for the curtain of bamboo that ringed the glade did not allow all of the sun through. Only the tips of the concrete crosses threw very short shadows on the green soft lawn.

Yet, standing in the late afternoon, it was the sensation of heat he remembered now. He saw his mother and himself moving, with the other mourning women and children, from cross to cross at twelve o'clock of Good Friday and felt the heat from the sun and the desire to escape from it into the small, stone chapel for the final prayers. He looked at the chapel now. It was inviting as it had always been and he began to move towards it. Then he stopped. A woman had arisen from one of the crosses on the farther side and was slowly walking to the next. He recognized her. He had been watching the slim straight figure walk, every morning at Mass when he was a boy, to receive Holy Communion. Now, as she moved before him, as if asleep, her eyes closed and her lips moving continually, he felt like a spy. He must have moved for she turned suddenly and opened her eyes. Her discovery of his presence embarrassed him.

"Mr Lestrade, Sir."

He had already gone down some steps. He stopped and turned. She was walking towards him. Her dress was too short and too big for her.

"Excuse me," she said, "for disturbing you like that."

"No, no," John said, "it's me who's disturbing you. I'm sorry."

"Mr Lestrade, Sir," she said, "I only call you to say accept my sympathy." She stretched her hand out and he took it briefly.

"Thanks, Miss Amélie," he said.

"I never forget her in my prayers," Miss Amélie said.

She spoke as if her voice were tired, and as thin and hardy as her body must be. She could not have been any less than sixty.

"You are kind," he said to her, feeling uncomfortable. "Thank you very much, Miss Amélie. I mustn't keep you from your prayers."

He turned to go. She placed her thin hand on his arm. The touch of her hand was disagreeable to him. Yet her hand was clean.

"And please, Sir," she said, "don't mind what people saying, you hear, Sir?"

He moved away from the closeness of her face. He wanted very much to go now.

"No, of course not. Goodbye."

"Mr Lestrade?"

He turned again, already two steps lower.

"You not buying a ticket, Sir?" She held a bunch of Irish Sweepstake tickets in her hand. Wanting to get away he bought one. But, before he left, she made him buy one of her holy pictures as well.

"Goodbye, Sir," she said, and there was the slightest edge, to her already thin voice, of her gratitude.

"Goodbye, Miss Amélie," John said, and went down the rest of the steps and back onto the asphalted heat of the road. He crumpled up the holy picture and threw it away. Miss Amélie had been praying and selling Sweepstake tickets for years. Every booklet she sold entitled her to two free tickets. She still sold tickets. And she still prayed.

The shouts of children playing in the Botanical Gardens on the lower side of the road made him look down. They were playing outside the tennis courts waiting for the tennis players to arrive. The lucky ones selected would be paid sixpence an hour. As he watched, a car, Anne-Marie's, stopped in front of the small pavilion next to the courts and Anne-Marie and Miriam came out of it. The children stopped playing and ran to the car. The girls began to play. Another girl arrived and Anne-Marie, who had been too good for Miriam alone, now played against the two of them. She was easily more than a match for them. Watching her as she moved he remembered her, the day of his mother's funeral, striding – like a stallion he had thought then – across the cemetery over to him. He was standing next to her car. Miriam had just left to go to look for Anne-Marie.

Earlier on he had not heard Miriam's footsteps when she came. Her voice had surprised him, though he had not turned to look at her.

"It's finished, John," she said, "everybody's left."

He did not try to get up from where he was sitting on the sand.

"I wish I could tell you how sorry I am," she said.

He smoked, his back against the coconut tree and to her, looking at the waves.

"Can I do anything to help?" she asked.

Her dress was being blown against her body by the same steady wind that had brought Stephen's cry to him. He said nothing.

"I know," she said. "Of course I cannot help. I'm sorry, John."

He turned and looked at her. Then looked back at the waves.

"Do you know what I was thinking just now?" she asked.

"Tell me," he said.

"They were putting the dirt over your mother's grave and I turned and looked around and I saw all those little crosses with names on them and their dearly beloveds. And I remembered Stephen. And I thought how strange that Stephen should not even have a grave to show that he had lived and died."

He said nothing.

"I hadn't thought of that before, you know. I'd been so busy forgetting."

John was silent.

"You know what I mean?" she asked.

"Yes."

"He wanted so much to be remembered. He was going to do so many things that would be permanent. Leave so many traces of himself behind."

"Yes."

"It is funny," she said. She sounded as if she had moved away. He knew she had not. He knew, equally, without turning to watch her, that she was looking no longer at him but at the sea.

"Yes," he said.

32

"And frightening."

Again he looked at her. Was it at this discovery that it all ended? And yet she seemed now, saying this, as composed as she had looked on that Sunday when he so much envied her her serenity.

"Very frightening," he said. He turned to look at the sea again.

"Yes," she said, "perhaps you're right."

"One does need to be strong, doesn't one?" she said again.

It seemed less a question than a statement. And he did not feel that it was made to him.

"Yes," he said, "one needs to be strong."

"But what does that mean, John," she asked, "to be strong?"

"One must be able to take it," he said, remembering his mother again and his anger beginning to rise. "One must accept. As you do."

"As I do?"

"One must not rebel. One must acquiesce. Bow down." He was definitely angry now.

"Can that be strength?" she asked.

"Well wasn't it for you? Doesn't the Church teach there can be no other? That we must accept God's will? Submit to it? Be crushed under the weight of it? Isn't that what you did?"

"I was tired and afraid. I told you so."

Suddenly he felt angry for being angry. It seemed so useless. Even as level-headed a girl as Miriam had not escaped. Perhaps, too, she had understood for she paid no heed to his anger.

"Forgive me," he said, getting to his feet.

"Don't think about it, John."

They went back to the grave, filled now and abandoned. In a side path Anne-Marie's car was alone. Miriam left him. Much of his anger had already dissipated when Anne-Marie strode over to him.

"Feeling better?" she asked, smiling.

"Confused," he said. He had been thinking throughout the funeral service: during the ride to the cemetery in the back of Anne-Marie's car, and, while they were filling the grave, under the coconuts where Miriam had disturbed him.

"Naturally," Anne-Marie said. "Cigarette?"

John accepted a cigarette and a light from her.

"People say the dead are lucky," she said. "They may not be, but they certainly are peaceful."

The late evening was spread all around them like something palpable to absorb sound. All shadow had gone with the sun and the true dark had not yet fallen. And, hanging on to the palpable dusk, there was the smell of the sea, of rotting flowers on other graves, and of the damp, freshly dug sand his mother lay under. His anger drained from him.

"You know you're being blamed, of course?" she said. She was nearly as tall as he was.

"I guessed. It was not too difficult."

Muriel, when she had told him of his mother's death, had hardly bothered to veil her accusations.

"It doesn't worry you, does it?"

A cow mooed. Its sound lingered. Without waiting for an answer Anne-Marie said, "Very appropriate."

"Yes," John said. "It doesn't worry me in the least. They don't understand."

"No. No, they don't. But they always behave as if they do. They wouldn't let you alone now, you know that?"

She should know. He said, "I don't care."

Then Miriam had arrived and, together, they had driven off.

In the car Anne-Marie said, "I forgot. Harold is coming back. Mr Montague told me so. Both he and Mrs Charles were looking for you, John. Mr Montague said to me, 'You know that boy coming back?' And I said something or other and he said, 'I hope he change that's all!'"

"He looks old," Miriam said.

"When's Harold coming back?" John asked.

"Next month I believe."

"Mrs Charles looks well," Miriam said.

"She does," said Anne-Marie.

John was sitting in the back of the car. In front of him Anne-Marie's neck, straight with her concentration on the road, was long and slender. Next to her, the top of Miriam's head just showed. The hair on it, unlike the smooth straightness of Anne-Marie's, was like strands of waxed, brown twine just unravelled.

"And so," Anne-Marie said, "another lawyer is coming home."

"Any news of Derek?" Miriam asked.

"They've got another baby, his mother said. Another boy. Mrs Charles made a joke of it, you know, for my benefit. It was I who asked for news, not she who offered it."

"She's nice," Miriam said. John imagined the pleasureful puckering of Miriam's face expressing her liking for someone or for something. The expression, enhancing the effect of her small stature, made her look even more like a child.

"Hasn't stopped calling me daughter-in-law," Anne-Marie said.

They were going down the last of the hills and were almost in the town now.

"Doesn't look as if Derek ever intends to come back," Miriam said. "It's nearly seven years isn't it?"

"Nearly," Anne-Marie said.

They were in the town.

"Where shall I drop you, Miriam?"

"Home," Miriam said, "there's something I must do."

"We shall have to do something for Harold," Miriam said, "a party or something."

The car stopped and Miriam got down from it.

"Say hello to your mother for me," John said.

"You understand she couldn't come to the funeral," Miriam said. "One of us had to stay at home."

"I know."

"You won't come in? Not even for a second?"

"Some other time."

As if impatient, Anne-Marie sparked the car. Miriam entered the house.

"See you tonight," she called out to Anne-Marie as she drove off. While Anne-Marie was waving her acknowledgment she said, "Sometimes I think he'd be better off dead. Don't you?"

He had often felt that way about his own mother. Now, already, so soon after her funeral, he wondered.

"You don't agree, I suppose," Anne-Marie said, for John had not answered.

"I suppose not. Not now anyway."

35

"Oh, of course. I wasn't very tactful. Still, to sit and look out of a window day after day. I don't know how Miriam can stand it. I couldn't."

"No?"

"Not even if he were my father."

John said nothing.

"And yet," she said, "I suppose I would have to. Isn't it disgusting how easily we adjust?"

They were in that part of the town where Derek had once lived and which a fire had destroyed a year before he left for England. After eight years some portions still had not been rebuilt. In the vacant lots the grass was high behind the concrete pavements and here and there a coconut- or a breadfruit-tree stood out of it. It was after the fire that Anne-Marie had met Derek.

"Don't you think so?" Anne-Marie prodded for John had said nothing.

"No, not particularly I hadn't."

"Well you will."

She sounded very sure.

"Like a drink?" she asked as they turned into the street on which she lived.

"I could do with one," he said.

They stopped at her house. It was Saturday and she had gone for an early game of tennis before the funeral and her tennis things were on the chairs and on the floor.

"Pay no attention to the pigsty," she said.

She went into the kitchen for the drinks. After her father's death Anne-Marie had sold the big house she and old D'aubain had lived in overlooking Columbus Square and had had this small one built for her. Apart from the kitchen there was the dining-sitting-room he was in now, a toilet and a bedroom.

Books were scattered all over. Records, in and out of their covers, lay all about. The chairs were not arranged and the plates and the remains of what must have been breakfast were still on the small dining table. It was as if the disorder in the room was the complement to the elegance and the efficiency that Anne-Marie was in public. He got up and put the Peer Gynt Suite on the turntable.

Anne-Marie came in with the drinks. There was a picture of Derek in his bachelor's gown on the wall and she saw him looking at it.

"Water or ginger?" she asked.

"Water."

"I'll just have the first one neat," she said. She sat down. "What were you thinking just now?" she asked.

John did not understand. Anne-Marie pointed to the framed picture of Derek smiling down upon them.

"Oh."

"You think I should take it down perhaps?"

She sipped her drink and smiled.

"I wasn't thinking any such thing," John protested.

"I suppose I should though," she said.

She sat holding her drink in both hands as if to warm it or warm her palms with it. Her legs were crossed and she was leaning forward slightly as she looked up at the picture. The music flowed around them.

"Anyway there's still time," she said.

"Do you have to remove it? I don't…"

"He's coming home too," she said smiling. She sat back in her chair.

"Derek?"

She nodded, smiling still.

"Mrs Charles told me so."

"You didn't mention it in the car."

"I wanted to keep the news to myself a little while first," she said. "I don't suppose he thought of writing to tell me."

"Is he coming together with Harold?"

Still smiling she shook her head, but slowly, as if, already, a part of her had moved forward into the future and, simultaneously, backward into the past.

"Derek'll be coming a month or so later," she said.

"Another lawyer," he said, mocking her.

She nodded, slowly and still smiling, and poured another drink for each of them. She sat down again.

"Yes," she said. "He'll come back. And everybody'll be looking."

"After so long?"

"Uh huh."

"No. Not after seven years."

"Maybe not. But I doubt it."

The music filled up the emptiness of the break in their conversation. They both had another drink.

"What are you going to do?" she asked.

John shrugged his shoulders.

"Did she have any property?"

"Only the house."

"You'll want to sell it, I suppose. Or rent it."

"I suppose."

He could not be bothered to go into those details. From quite near the cathedral clock sounded the half-hour.

"Half past six."

"I thought it was later."

"Are you hungry?" she asked. "I didn't have lunch. We can share it."

The record had come to an end. Anne-Marie went into the kitchen to warm the lunch.

"I need a servant, John," she said throwing her voice, "can't survive without one. Will you clear the table, please?"

Her little excursion into the past and present had ended. She was all present again. John took the dirty things into the kitchen and brought out the dishes she gave him. She hardly ate. He, a great deal. While he was eating she removed the record and put on a calypso. She poured herself another drink.

"You don't have to go away unless you want to," she said. "You can sleep here."

"I think I'll go home."

"Sure you want to be alone up there tonight?"

"Sure."

He left the table at which he was eating and joined her in the sitting room proper. He poured himself a drink.

"Like to have the rest?" she offered.

"I'm stocked."

"O.K. Whenever you're ready."

"Thanks Anne-Marie. I want to walk."

"At least you can leave your jacket here and your tie."

"Good idea. Thanks."

He began to walk to his home on the hill. He had wished, walking along the carefully chosen streets, more than anything else, to be alone with the mixture of relief and pain that his mother was affording him. He tried to imagine her dead. But the image of the sick woman, alive, in the white nightgown, the long, black face drawn tightly over the bones under the line of the short greying hair, was that of someone he had known a very long time ago.

Standing now on the edge of the road he watched Anne-Marie and the other girls as they played. He had not seen either Anne-Marie or Miriam since the day of his mother's funeral.

He continued to walk down the hill. The road curved for the last time then straightened to form a street on the edge of the town. The trees on his left gave place to small wooden houses, mostly new, some as yet unfinished. He turned right and entered the Botanical Gardens. Because of the canopy of trees it was darker and, as it had been in the shadow of the bamboo on the edge of the sanctified glade, cooler. Miss Amélie's face and its despairing confidence while she prayed came again to him. The anger, too, and the understanding. She would pray thus until she died; and she would die, perhaps more quickly, if she did not pray. Yet for her, as it had been for his mother, to die surely was the ultimate Salvation. The life which she wrapped in borrowed clothes that did not always fit and capped with her Sweepstake tickets and the resigned expectancy her religion taught her, was only a point of departure. Like a railway station. Or like a wharf. Death was the ship she would sail on. And death was precisely what she, as his mother had done on her sick bed for three years, would fight against all her life.

He walked on. The sound of birds returning to their nests high up in the gru-gru palms was all about him. He left the gardens for the brighter light of the open, unpaved space and walked along one of the filthy canals to the sea's edge. The fisherman's canoes idled in the moving water. He read some names, GOD WILL PROVIDE, HOPE, IN GOD WE TRUST. The smell of filth was mixed with the fresh smell of fish and the smell of the sea. He turned left away from the groups of fishermen and women and followed the line of the wharf proper now where the schooners rested and the water was deep. He moved past the unmistakable accents of sailors from the other islands, past the empty space where the steamers normally berthed, the sea open now to his right, and stretching flatly, between the embrace of the headlands, out to the very small harbour mouth in the distance. The sea here was clean only without the fresh scent of fish or the dirty smell of the canals. But across it, where the river that flowed behind the town ended in a small estuary along the base of the left promontory of the harbour, the water was dirty and the discarded bits of cotton and lint, with red patches where the sores had bled, floated on it. Behind the old dispensary the smoke from the burning rubbish rose; there was the strong smell of medicine, the smell of burning and unburnt rubbish, and the less assertive, more general smell of the estuary itself. As a boy he had often stood in the dirty, shallow water, his shoes in his hands and the unclean smells all around him, looking at the rats drown in their submerged cages. The frantic struggle of the rats to escape amused him. They clung to the steel wires. They fought each other for possession as if the wires did not confine them to death but led to liberty and life. They bit one another. They turned their sharp teeth even on themselves. He and his friends watched and laughed. Eventually, exhausted, they lost their grip and sank slowly, their grey bellies upturned, and the displaced air from their bodies rising in assorted bubbles to the sea's dirty surface. He moved from cage to cage, happy, pointing out gleefully to his friends those rats which resisted the longest and whose spasms in the water continued for long after those of the others had already ceased. And afterwards, when not a single one of them moved except in that slow, indeterminate movement that the sea transmitted to its lifeless, curved body, he had felt regret as at the too-quick end to an entertainment. But, like all things, he had, with time, forgotten them. It had only been later that he remembered them again.

He left the wharf and went through the business section of the town, closed now and quiet after work. He crossed the bridge over the river and walked past the police station where, after Stephen's death, he had concocted his statement and up the hill which climbed steeply. He walked with his head down, wanting to see nobody, missing the relative emptiness of the wharf and of the business part of the town for there were people here on the road. The sun had gone down, the lingering heat was beginning to be not unpleasant, and the people were preparing for the evening meal. On either side of the road he was aware of the small wooden houses he did not look at. The sound of voices and of feet was about and the sound of water falling, and of buckets, made him look briefly as he went past the standpipe. Quickly, in order to leave them behind, he climbed. He walked uphill for about ten minutes. Then going around one of the many hairpin turns of the very steep road he saw the town in the valley below him and the flat harbour and the ships like toys and the long outflung arm of the promontory on the northern side of the harbour and, beyond that, the wide expanse of the Caribbean breaking in white distant lines on the strip of beach. The town lay in squares and the hills almost encircled it and, here and there, the red top of a house showed through the green. Along the rectangular streets of the town cars moved distantly, as on a film, without noise, and he could see the Botanical Gardens on the far side of the town and the ribbon of the road that went beyond it past the glade where he had surprised Miss Amélie.

She must still be there, he thought, remembering his mother even more strongly now and seeing again her still, shawled figure hunched in the middle of the bed, murmuring her prayers in the semidark of the sputtering flame. The faded pictures of saints behind it on the shelf were grimy with accumulated dust and the excreta of flies, and the small images of Christ and the Virgin Mary, whose stone limbs had been mutilated by repeated fallings over the years, seemed to waver behind the flickering flame. His child's eyes open, and afraid of the shapes of clothes that lurked behind the door, he lay quietly in the bed, already fascinated by his mother's quiet figure, unwilling to disturb, cultivating even then the feeling he had had so strongly in the glade, of embarrassment, when Amélie had turned to look at him.

He thought that the nights he awoke and did not see her thus must have been very few indeed. John did not think that the night his father came to the house had been one of them. He was not sure that the incident really happened. That one night while his mother was praying in the half dark or perhaps had fallen asleep in her attitude of prayer, he, awake but pretending he was not, had heard his father knock on the front door of the house until it seemed he would break down both the wooden door as well as his mother's resolution not to answer. He was not sure for at a very early age he had begun, because he knew so little, to invent stories about his parents and sometimes he could not know afterwards where reality had ended and his imagination had begun. If it did really happen, then it must have been because of him, asleep as she thought, that his mother had finally come down from the bed and gone to open the front door.

Had he heard, "Go to your wife?" or had he imagined it later? It is possible that lying in the semidark, his eyes closed because he was alone, he had heard his mother say, "You don't have no right to come here now. And you making all that noise, too. You think I don't have shame?"

His father's voice, which he had never heard except during the day, was strange against the quiet of the night.

"You don't think you give the neighbours enough to say already?" his mother asked. And he imagined, remembering now, the defiance and the hurt pride that peeped from behind the question she asked.

"You have your wife. You have no right here." It was a whisper, for his benefit.

But the night was quiet and the whisper floated over the wooden walls to his sleepy ears.

His father began to speak. She interrupted him. "You making too much noise. You want to wake up the child?"

After that he heard little for he was falling asleep. Once only, the sound of that strange new voice rose sufficiently to pierce his drowsiness.

"You too proud, Lena. Your pride will kill you."

He must have fallen asleep. When he awoke, she was there, as usual, sitting in the bed murmuring her prayers as if she had never been disturbed.

John walked slowly up the hill. The green on either side of the road was unbroken for long periods by the large stone houses of those who could afford to build here. All the images of his mother were of her alive for he had refused to look upon her dead face.

He had known that her quiet, suffocating concern for him after Stephen's death was stilled forever. Their wordless fights consisting of looks only and of the pain and the helplessness of each to reach the other could no longer take place. But it was as if he feared that, lying in the coffin, the long, tired face might raise a black eyelid briefly in a wink of reproach. And he had not dared. He had had an overwhelming feeling of joy, for her, that she was dead and of liberation, for himself, that the symbol she increasingly became of his own helplessness no longer existed. Her ship of life had berthed and she would alight somewhere transcendentally light and, he hoped, somehow, happy.

During the funeral service he had sat alone, not praying, enclosed in a little circle of grief not for her death but for the way she had lived. In the comparative dark of the vaulty church he was filled with a sense of wasted effort. He regretted, while the priest and the acolytes chanted at the altar and the bells tolled, that his mother had chosen not to live her life alone, that she had dared to sacrifice for another even though that other were her own son; that he had been unable to accept the contract she offered. He was sorry that neither his father nor himself had given her the companionship she had hoped for. And he was glad that her wasted effort, unrewarded, had come to an end.

But even before they had begun to carry the coffin out of the church his gladness was already tinged with a sense of loss. He would never look upon his mother's face again. Nor could he ever give her any satisfaction of his success. He knew then that his overwhelming desire for achievement had been as much for her as it had been for him. That achievement, which he was about to set out for, was to have been the bouquet he would place at her feet, to let her hold with her calloused hands and to look upon with her tired eyes, to caress if she still remembered how. And it was for this reason that when Stephen's cry had come to him on the beach the day before their departure he had not dared to respond to it.

His own dead body had seemed to be borne with that cry on the same wind and the stench of it had entered all his pores at once so that, in his fear, he had stood transfixed and had looked at, but not seen, the figure of his friend struggling in the water before him.

2

John left the climbing, pitched road and moved, still upwards, along the path that led to the shelf where the barracks he lived in were. The path was even steeper than the road had been and he was forced to walk more slowly. He did not mind. The path was the private road that led to his home. It was narrow and he was secure between its green walls. The smell of damp and the many sounds of the undergrowth were familiar. The sky was only a thin line above the twisting path.

There was a light in his room. Muriel, his mother's friend and the wife of the old caretaker of the barracks, had already brought supper. He went inside, closing the door behind him, and shut the window against insects. His clothes now hung from nails in the wall above his cot. There was a clean sheet on the cot and the chair was pushed neatly under the small wooden table. The game of chess he had hoped to return to was destroyed. Muriel had collected the pieces into their box which was now in the very middle of the folded cardboard. John sat on the edge of the cot and began to eat out of the single bowl his meal was in.

"It was all you wanted, to go away. Always that was what you wanted. And what I wanted because you wanted it."

That was what his mother had said when he had been forced to tell her he no longer wished to go to Canada. She was in the middle of the bed; it was here that she had ended after her sudden collapse in the small shop, as if to complete, in the same place, the circle that had begun with his first awareness of her. Over her head the canopy, supported by the four varnished bedposts, sagged under the weight of accumulated dust. She sat under it, sick and worried, like a queen of despair. The sputtering of the small lamp, and the Holy Images it never ceased to burn before, were her only heralds.

"I don't want it now. I can't want it now," he said.

"I do not understand," she said. Her voice alone moved as if it groped over the halfdark between them to reach him faintly.

"What's the matter, John?" she asked. She had wished to ask this repeatedly since Stephen's death, observing him.

He said, "Nothing." It was the stock answer. But he added, "Please, Ma, you must leave me alone."

The diminutive, so rarely used to inflict pain, sounded strange to him.

"I want to help," she said.

There was no need for her assertion. But help was the last thing he needed now. His sense of personal unworthiness was more intense than that which he had felt as a boy waiting to enter the confessional. His penance, as it had been then, would have to be performed by him alone.

"You cannot help, Ma."

"If I cannot, John, then who else?"

And then the inflexibility of her attitude, which she could not change because she did not know, had irked him. Her love and her concern sprang out at him and he recoiled. It was not the protection of love he wanted but the reason of understanding. He must pay. Otherwise he could never look upon himself again.

"What are you punishing yourself for, John?" she asked.

He would have liked to expose everything, not to her love, but to her understanding, not to her sympathy but to her admiration. He was like a monk being flagellated and yearning for the silent admiration of those who beat him.

"Why are you punishing yourself?" she asked again for he had not answered.

"What do you mean?" he prevaricated.

"You're punishing yourself. And you're punishing me. Whatever you're punishing yourself for, you're punishing me, too, for it."

It was intolerable that she should take his pain and add to hers.

It was intolerable that he should have pain she could not share.

They were compelled to a confrontation neither of them had looked for.

Genuinely he said, "I'm sorry, I didn't mean…"

"Then go," she interrupted.

It was like a hiss.

"Go," she said, "for my sake if not for yours. Give me what I have waited for." Any means seemed desirable; and deceit, if it served, was not to be spurned. But to him it was blackmail. And it was ugly and despicable. Then he thought again and believed he saw the ruse behind it. The sympathy that elicited it sickened him. In both cases she was intruding now.

"You must leave me alone," he said gently, compulsorily, "to make my own decisions."

She did not speak to him again. But before the manifestations, so obvious to her, so hidden he thought, of his unease, she began to fear the worst. She suspected him of something even fouler than he had accused himself of. And, silenced by his attitude, and by the increasing sense she had that her fear was justified, she watched him only. She had been many things to him. Now he had shut her out and her eyes were the only window into the closed house he had become.

The quiet, sad intensity of their gaze was a perpetual reproach. For days he avoided her. But it was as if her gaze pierced the wooden walls of his small room. He was extremely aware of it. And in the end he could only flee.

John finished eating and went outside to get away from the heat of the closed room and to smoke. The dark of the night was comfortable about his shoulders. He was like a warrior who had fought several battles in very quick succession and was, exhausted, resting now. He had not won, neither had his adversary lost. But, now, it was unlikely that he would ever fight again. The shock at his discovery of an essential ugliness, even though the sadness that he could never run away from it remained, had turned to fascination; his shame to a sort of wonder. From his memory he had exhumed corpses of his old self, probing them with the scalpel of his new awareness, lifting his motives delicately out of their integuments to look at them. He had felt very very fragile and absolutely dangerous. He had been like an archaeologist collecting fossils to recreate a future only. But the timidity and the fear his discovery of himself had instilled and the paralysis they induced made any reconstruction in the future too daring for him to contemplate.

It was to the lived, happier memories of his past that he had looked instead. Many afternoons he had lain on his cot, naked, the sheet wet with his perspiration, while, in dreams, they came back to him. And when he awoke, the images still in his mind, and looked at the unpainted ceiling, he would have wished, but for the discomfort of the heat and the wetness under his body, to will himself to sleep again.

In nearly all of them Rose had been.

Rose.

It was only now that her memory was sharp. Even when, already, it had stood apart from the memories of the other women in his life, even though she had not been just another face to the paper cut-out they all had been, he had remembered her with a pleasure that was only faintly nostalgic, and without regret. The pleasure had changed. The regret only was new.

He had met Rose five years ago when he went to Grenada with the island's cricket team. She lived almost on the very edge of a small beach so windy that hardly anything could remain on the table in the sitting room without being blown down. There was nothing in it except some chairs, the table in the centre, and a few pictures hanging on the wall, never still, making a continuous small noise against their conversation. But there were potted plants on the verandah that ran around the house and an excellent small garden, full of flowers, at the back. He had spent a part of almost every day there after he had met Rose. The appearance of complete harmony in this family of six, materially well-off (her father was Examiner of Accounts), impressed him. There was a gracefulness in the plump, black woman who served him and who, judging from the number and the ages of her children, must have been older than she looked, that contrasted with the prematurely old, almost fierce activity of his own mother. There was much laughter from the girls, Rose's younger sisters, some pleasant banter from her mother; and her brother, the youngest of the family, wore his cricket cap and imitated him. It had been as much for the feeling of belonging to a family as for the genuine pleasure of Rose's company that he had continued, all during his stay, to frequent the little, salt-sprayed bungalow near the sea.

With Rose the precocious sexual aggressiveness that was a tradition in his own island and which he had learnt very easily had dropped away from him like a worn skin. Not once had he even tried to kiss her. Her accent, her laughter, the mere fact of her presence with him, alone, satisfied him. He had not needed to touch her. She was there next to him and he could listen to her, watch her. He looked much at her. She was strange and unlike any woman he had met before. Any girl, that is, for she was still at school, in the final year of the Sixth. And he had been hesitant and, for once, almost shy.

It had been in their letters after he had returned to his own island that the explosion of feeling had taken place. Each letter had been a promise. Each a stone placed on the last and awaiting the next, erecting the structure of his and her happiness together. In the end it had been the aspect of promised solidity their letters had put up that had frightened him. His decision to get away from a life which, resumed, was oppressive as ever, could not include Rose now. He had, simply, to put her out of his mind.

He wanted the opposite of the solidity that Rose seemed to offer him. He wanted relationships that were as ephemeral and transitory as his existence was, relationships that could afford him the temporary pleasure he looked for while he was marking time on the island.

He had formed plenty of them. Every year young women were leaving secondary school to work in the Service or, if they were fair enough in skin, in one of the island's banks. The education they had received had prepared them for very little else. One or two went to universities abroad. The majority stayed at home on the island. They could not all become the wives of the few professional men who returned, unmarried, from England or America. Because of the education they had received they would not marry policemen nor the small struggling businessman who, more often than not, had not been to secondary school. And the young civil servant who, like himself, was only waiting to accumulate money, did not often marry them. They formed friendships, therefore, which they believed to be secret, more or less precarious, unprotected by law, unsanctioned by religion, and discussed by everybody. Contraceptives and, less often, abortion, assured their respectability and their freedom.

Within the island's context, therefore, it had not been difficult for him to forget Rose. Or so he had thought. For, in her sudden, unexpected appearance on another island, after two years of silence, he had felt immediately all of his previous sensations again. If, in the interval, he had forced himself to forget the quick, quiet smile, the bit of hair over the broad forehead, and the pleasure seeing her had given him before, he found them all again in the young womanliness that was established now, and in the poise with which, as if unaffected by the surprise of their meeting, she turned from the counter of the small store to look at him. He had known again, and all of a sudden, the same quiet excitement that she had filled him with three years ago and, for him, it was, immediately, as if they had never stopped writing, as if he had never tried to forget her, as if they had planned to meet in this small store, unexpectedly.

He had been surprised at the beauty of her body, when, on the day before she left for her own island, she stepped, in her bathsuit, from behind the seagrape. Often he was to see her in memory as she was then, smiling, the hair over the forehead disarranged, and the yellow bathcap, flung, coming across the hot air at him.

They bathed in the clear shallow water that scarcely rippled, so calm it was. She seemed happy. He had never been happier. Yet, already, the happiness had seemed not to be quite real. It was as if he were dreaming and aware, as sometimes the sleeper is aware before awakening, that it was only a dream. They made love. She had not made love before. But she gave herself to him confidently even if inexpertly. Afterwards they sat on the sand and smoked. The subdued exhilaration for him after the act of love, Rose's presence on the sand next to him, perhaps, too, the unfamiliarity of the beach – everything seemed to suggest an unreality he was imagining only.

And then she spoke.

"I hope this time you won't stop writing," she said.

It seemed a statement. He knew it was a question and did not

49

want to answer it. She, obviously, expected him to. He could have promised he would write. It would have saved him and her a great deal. But he had been too happy to try and perpetuate his happiness by a lie.

He said, "There seems to be little point, Rose."

She looked as if his answer had been an irrelevance and he still had to reply to the question she had asked.

"We are happy now," he said, "very happy. But afterwards. I don't know."

She did not speak at once. She seemed to be trying to get at the hidden meaning behind the anagram of words he had used.

Then she said, "I don't understand, John."

The feeling as of a dream was stronger. He would have liked to awake.

She threw her cigarette away. He was thinking, if only I could have avoided this.

"Have you been playing games with me again?" she asked.

The memory of his so recent happiness was receding rapidly. He wished, sitting in the heat, that a fairy would come and wave a wand and he would awake, sighing with relief and yet with disappointment, that the spell was over. She placed her towel over her. It seemed to him the gesture of a naked woman before a man she did not know.

He said, "You know I'm going to Canada for seven years."

"So?"

"Seven years," he repeated. "Seven years. You realize what can…?"

"What?" she asked. She was curt. It made her seem new. Her strangeness accentuated the feeling of unreality.

"What is it I must realize, John?" she asked again when he had not answered.

"Can we start anything and continue seven years later?"

"Oh, John," she said, "didn't we after three?"

It seemed an eternity before he answered her. Her insistence, already, was beginning to irritate him. The cigarettes he smoked were tasteless and he felt he was in something unpleasant he would like to get away from.

"Rose," he said as if he were tired, "seven years are a long time."

50

"Why should they make a difference?" she asked.

"But they do, Rose, don't you see?"

"No, I don't. I don't think they make a difference at all."

"I think it's unfair…"

"Unfair to whom?" she interrupted him. And then, "To you?"

He pretended he had not felt the slight prick of her disdain. He said, "No. To you."

They were quarrelling.

"I see," she said.

"So many things can happen in seven years," he said. "How can you wait…?"

"Now," she said, "I know I can."

He said very quietly, "I see."

"No, you don't. You don't see anything at all."

"Don't I? You seemed to have made it only too clear."

"How stupid," she said. "You're wrong. I didn't mean it as you think."

She was hurt at his interpretation. He was not sure that she didn't despise him for it. He was sorry, too, now. But the hidden fear it had disturbed could not make distinctions of nicety. She was explaining however.

She said, "What I meant, John, was that now, after this second meeting, not after a while ago, I know that seven years cannot make a difference. I had felt; now I am sure."

She had meant to reassure him. And to change whatever his interpretation might have suggested to him of her. But she had already disturbed his fear; her determination now drove it hysterically around his mind.

"I will not allow you to," he said, and his hysteria, although quiet, was very real. "It's not fair. I… cannot."

Thinking about it later he knew he had really meant unfair to himself, not to her. But he had not realized he was prevaricating when he said to Rose, "I want you to be happy. I want to give you the chance to get the happiness you deserve, whenever it comes, if it does, within the seven years. I don't want to be an obstacle to you in any way."

"And I?" she had wanted to know, "don't I have a say in my own happiness?"

Her remark was just. He had been inflicting her happiness upon her as if it were a gift, his gift.

"I want you to be free to choose it when it comes."

"But can't you see?" she was almost shouting. "I have chosen."

She seemed about to continue, then to change her mind. He said nothing. As if for the first time he was aware of the sun on his back, of the increased noises of the sea. He realized he had been squinting at the glare.

"Don't you?"

He did not answer. There was only the heat and the glare; and the discomfort of his dry body under the sun.

"I can wait for seven years if you can."

He wanted, suddenly, to end it at once.

"It's a waste of time," he said. "I want you to be free," he said again, "I want you to be free to lead your life in the interval. And I want to be free too."

He had said it, almost without realizing, driven by his impatience. But he had said it and she had understood.

"Free?" she wondered as if to herself. "You're free, John, don't let me hold you. Only…"

She did not finish.

"Only what?"

"Oh, never mind." Then shaking her head slowly and almost whispering, she said, "You're so selfish. You think only of yourself."

Irritated, he had wanted to ask whether she, too, were not also being selfish and thinking of herself only. But he had become tired of their conversation and did not wish to prolong it. The old wall had sprung up between them. It was mossy with age and covered with dirt, but it was as solid as it had ever been. And it was about to separate them forever. It was the wall of human selfishness and misunderstanding, of imperfectly explained and imperfectly understood motives and, though they might have been able to get over it singly, they could never, together, scramble over its ugly top.

He said, after a while, "Rose, please try to be reasonable."

He did not know what he could have meant by that. She could have told him the same thing with the same absence of meaning. Between them words were a waste of time.

She said, "All right, John, I'm very reasonable now."

She had been getting up even as she was speaking and stood now, her bath cap at her feet. He picked it up and handed it to her.

They drove back, in a taxi, through a drizzle that was cold and depressing, to her Guide camp. And her letter when it came, had given him some pleasure. "Perhaps, and in spite of you, we may meet again. Since our last meeting I have thought a great deal. I have arrived at nothing I did not think or feel before. It's no use. And I've tried, unsuccessfully to be reasonable. My engagement, as you must have heard, lasted only three months. Maybe I do not know how to be reasonable. But I know now what you once told me; everything changes with time. Already the outlines of our last meeting are blurred and I have difficulty when I try to remember to see it clearly. But still I remain convinced, dear John, (forgive this) that you were wrong, completely wrong. Unless, of course, you had been fooling me all the time. But I don't believe you were. To do so you would have to be capable of the greatest duplicity and I don't think you are."

3

How right she was, John thought, when she wrote that he was wrong, and how justified in thinking that he might have been deceiving her. Yet the thought, that the possibility of his deceit, which she said she had not considered seriously, had crossed her mind, hurt him. For Rose still remained the only woman that he had ever loved.

"You're so selfish," she had said, "you think only of yourself."

In his imagination he confronted her once more and was ashamed. And because to have lost her, to have given her up, and to regret it now was very painful he consoled himself by thinking that, for her, it had been good he had been wrong. He had been right when he gave her up because subsequent events had proved, only too clearly, that he had not deserved her.

Rose's letter had arrived almost a year after their last meeting and only a few weeks before Stephen and himself were to leave the island to go to Canada. He had detached himself from Rose or from anything that happened to her. Their relationship had ended and there was nothing to be done. Only occasionally he removed it from the drawer of his memory and looked at it with some delight and a curiosity, quite pleasant, about how things might have been. The news that the letter gave of her scholarship and her going to England to study Economics had merely been another topic for conversation when he mentioned it to Stephen that afternoon.

"Oh," Stephen said, "when did you hear?"

"The letter came today," John said.

"Well." Stephen put away the exercise books he had been correcting when John arrived and fetched the goblet of water and the bottle of French rum he kept mostly for John's benefit while they played chess. John took the glasses from the top of the safe in the corner. It was a ritual they performed almost every day. They placed the rum, water and glasses on the table on the verandah next to the unopened chessboard.

"This calls for a celebration," Stephen said. He poured out the drinks.

"I suppose so," John said without enthusiasm.

Stephen sat down at his end of the table with his drink. He made no attempt to set the chessboard. It was usually the first thing he did. Sometimes John arrived to find the board set and Stephen waiting for him. John sat down.

"To Rose," Stephen said, "to you and Rose. Cheers."

"To Rose anyhow," John said, "and to her success."

"You don't seem particularly happy."

John shrugged his shoulders.

"You should go to England, John," Stephen said.

John, who had been looking down from the verandah at the plump young civil servant who passed every day after work followed by the same two or three young men whom she juggled and whom she seemed always to give so much pleasure to, looked at Stephen.

"Whatever for?" he asked.

"For Rose," Stephen said, "what else?"

It was just another of Stephen's pranks. He looked down at the young woman and her attendant young men. He knew their gestures and the sounds they made almost by heart. He had been observing them for months now.

"I'm serious," Stephen said.

He seemed to be. His bespectacled black face was solemn. But John knew that no one could be as funny as Stephen nor, being funny, keep as straight a face. He smiled.

"Let's have a game," he said, beginning to take the chess pieces from the box they were in. But surprisingly, Stephen refused to play.

"I shouldn't hesitate if I were you," Stephen said.

"Wouldn't you?" John asked, not quite sure what to say.

"No, I wouldn't."

"Not even now?"

"Not even now."

John decided that his friend was serious. He could not understand why.

"And if Rose has changed?" he asked.

"You know she hasn't."

"How do I know that, Stephen?"

Even as he asked the question, they appeared. The young man had a parcel in one hand and held the arm of his new wife with the other. They stopped before their caged parrot. They had appeared neither too soon nor too late and their performance with the parrot seemed neither longer nor shorter than it had been yesterday or it would be tomorrow. They went inside, smiling as the man said something to her. John felt a pang of envy and of admiration for the young clerk who had had the courage so early to get married.

"She wrote you, didn't she?" Stephen asked.

"Yes, she did."

"So what more do you want?"

It was not normally like Stephen to be so insistent.

"You realize to go to England now is to lose another year. I couldn't possibly gain admission now."

"To lose a year now and gain how many years afterwards?" Stephen asked.

And now the last of John's automatons appeared, on time, old, in a suit, a pipe in its mouth and a briefcase bulging with papers under its arm. John sometimes felt that Mr Jackson would die and the briefcase would continue to hop along the path on its own.

"You'd be making an investment, John," Stephen said.

He had already made his. Miriam and Stephen were engaged to be married. Stephen had even been prepared to marry Miriam and leave her behind on the island. The many cases in the past of the results of separation and the glaring example of Anne-Marie high and dry on the broken limb of her engagement with Derek, married now in England, could not shake his conviction. Stephen was without doubt and the future belonged to him. Once only he had lifted his head from an already dedicated isolation that marked him apart from the rest of his friends on the island. He had seen Miriam floundering bravely in the backswell of her father's catastrophe and had chosen her. Slowly, out of their mutual shyness, their relationship had evolved, over a long time, from Stephen's initial discovery of her simplicity and grace at Mass, through unplanned brief meetings outside of the church, past a smile of recognition, repeated, in the streets, more assuredly through Anne-Marie's mutual friendship until, out of these and other hesitant stitches, the strong fabric of their own friendship had revealed itself.

"What's a year when there're so many to follow?" he asked. "For Miriam's sake I could put off going to University indefinitely."

Yet, four years ago, at Harold's farewell party, John had found him outside crying alone in the dark and beating the side of the wooden kitchen with his fists while inside, and under the bright lights, their friends were singing "For Auld Lang Syne" to Harold.

"I would wait," Stephen said, "for Miriam's sake. I wouldn't do it for anything else, of course."

John, pouring himself another drink and not really listening to Stephen, thought that he, too, like the civil servant and the clerk and the young married couple, was an automaton. Evening after evening he came here to play chess and drink. There was a key in his back as there were keys in the backs of all the inhabitants of the island. And those keys, it was the island itself that manipulated them. Thank God he was, at last, going away.

To get away. His glass in his hand, he looked up at the hills. Whenever he was tired of looking at the robots around him and of feeling himself one he looked at the hills. Their green steeply rising sides closed upon him. He imagined himself caught between the semicircle of hills as they closed in and being slowly crushed by them.

"…I would do it for nothing else," he heard the end of Stephen's sentence as if he had just entered the room. John was struck by the impression as of deliberately articulated speech. But Stephen's face and his entire attitude were calm and relaxed. The feeling as of clenched teeth or of tightly closed fists was in John's mind only.

"Shall we have a game now?" John asked.

Stephen shook his head.

"I'd only lose," he said.

He disliked intensely to lose. He was too careful to lose often.

If he did he said nothing. But without the slightest change in his countenance or outward stiffening of his manner he prepared immediately for the next game. He did not often lose it. Once they had played until nearly one in the morning because John had won the first game and Stephen who blamed himself and was eager for revenge would not let him go.

His refusal to play convinced John that something was wrong. And remembering Stephen's allusion to Miriam he asked.

"How's Miriam?"

"Miriam's fine," Stephen said, "there's nothing wrong with her."

"What's the matter then?"

"Nothing," Stephen said evenly and quietly. John felt the control. The impression, now, was not in his mind alone.

He would talk about it, John knew, only when he wished to. He watched as, along the path, people were moving up and down. They seemed content. Out of sight a woman, busy at some task, was singing as if she were not aware that she was doing so. The light had become soft. In it the small houses under rusty galvanized roofs stood, like the people who walked before them, as if with contentment. The contentment of acceptance. Only the children, playful and noisy, were unrestrained. Their shouts were loud and robust and the singing of the woman, out of sight, sounded anaemic by comparison.

"Let's go for a walk," Stephen said.

They had not been for a walk in months. Many evenings they had walked in the late light along the empty road that led to the beach. Sometimes they walked through the cemetery from the paupers' end where the graves were unmarked mounds of sand, past the wooden crosses, past the concrete and occasionally marble tombs of the very rich and out to the road at the other end which led back to the town. John remembered those walks with a pleasure that was a little sad. Often in the quiet cemetery, a cow grazing on the mound of hill beyond it, and the light soft after the harshness of the sun, he had felt contentment as if the impatience he carried within his breast was lulled, in the soft light and in the quiet, by the noise of the sea that seemed hardly to disturb it. Remembering them much later he thought they must have been extremely soothing to his friend's spiritual restlessness. His own he had been able to cover with the cloak of his several affairs, his drinking and his acceptance of pleasure under any of the forms that he found it. But Stephen's had burned steadily like a little light within the darkness of himself, intensely, silently. Only once, the night of Harold's party, had it shown its unflickering flame.

John got up at his friend's suggestion, poured himself another quick drink and followed Stephen down the stony unpaved path. They came to the tarred road and followed it out of town. Moving in the opposite direction, a few people, mainly women and children, were going to Rosary and Benediction. Faintly, from the centre of the town, the church bells called out to them.

John and Stephen moved along the road made dark already, at six o'clock, by the overhanging breadfruit trees that lined it. It was narrow with deep ruts and holes and, before long, an unpaved but wide track leading into the country. Stephen, his hands in his pockets, was kicking a stone before him, following it to the grassy edge of the road and back again into the centre. John lit a cigarette and smoked while he waited. The stone went to the side of the road where the grass was high and Stephen did not follow it. He fell in step again beside John. John, waiting as he walked, found his friend's silence intolerable. He knew that Stephen had something to say, and his expectation and Stephen's obvious reluctance made him uneasy. It was very quiet on the road. Only the sound of their feet on the gravel, and of the trees, barely moving, accompanied them. A mouse began quickly to cross the road ahead of them, reached the middle, then turned and scurried back to the side it had come from. Stephen, his head down, his hands in his pockets, began again to kick a stone. Then he laughed.

"My father," he said, and he was smiling, "is broke. He will not be able to pay back the money I lent him. My father said to me, 'You won't have to wait too long, Stephen, only a year.' That was what he said, 'only a year.'"

John remembered Stephen's distress when his father had asked for the second loan almost a year ago. He said nothing. He did not know what to say. The gloom under the trees had increased as the trees became more numerous. Already one or two fireflies were showing, and the night noises of insects, like the noises of a faulty radio turned low, were beginning to be heard. Stephen laughed. In the dark John could not see his face. It did not matter. Stephen's face hardly ever gave anything away.

John had learnt this during the sudden school assembly the very first week he had gone to St. Mary's College. While the English headmaster had spoken of honour and courage and the higher call of duty, and afterwards, recited the *De Profundis* for the repose of the souls of the two Old Boys shot down that week over Germany, Stephen had stood, his head unbowed, no trace of anything on his face. It was only much later that John, who had been standing next to him, had found out that one of the dead boys, the black one, had been Stephen's brother.

"Looks like I'll have to swim for it now," Stephen's voice said out of the dark.

"Don't you have any money at all, Stephen?" John asked.

"Not enough," Stephen said. "And then there's Miriam."

"Miriam will understand, surely?"

The dark had fallen truly now. Litanies of fireflies glowed. John and Stephen turned back.

"You know," Stephen said, "he must have known. He just didn't care. It didn't matter. What I was trying to do did not mean a thing to him."

John went to look at the schooner the next day. It was already launched and lay idling in the water. It looked very big indeed. But it had no masts, no cabins, nothing. Except the unfinished roughness of its hulk riding the small waves. It was obvious that work had stopped completely. John wondered what the old captain had done with Stephen's money and that which he had earned over the years of plying people's vessels among the islands before he had decided to build his own. His inspection over, he was watching the animation on the sea's edge when, from just behind him, the voice of Stephen, whom he had not heard approach, made him start.

"I can't understand what he could have done with all that money," it said.

John turned.

Stephen was saying quietly as he looked at his father's vessel, "I can't understand it."

The big unpainted shell of the schooner rose and fell ponderously and moved from side to side.

"Something is worrying Stephen," Miriam said to John once, "and he won't tell me what it is."

"And I can't," John had thought, to whom alone Stephen had confided his distress.

"Do you know what it is?"

"I don't," he lied. "I don't suppose it's anything serious."

"He's worried though. Even I can see that."

"It's probably the news," he said.

"What news?"

"About Desmond. They were great friends."

"It's already two weeks," she said.

"They were good friends. And you know how Stephen feels about things like that."

And Miriam, only a little reassured, had gone away.

As a practical joker and a prankster Desmond had almost been equal to Stephen. When the news of his death, in France where he had gone to fulfil a vocation for the priesthood that he had always hidden behind his ever-smiling face, had reached the island, there was a general expression of sorrow mixed with surprise. Stephen, however, had seemed less sorrowful than questioning, less surprised than baffled.

Death, especially of the young, had always preoccupied him. The death of the old he accepted but, for those who died under thirty, it was, for him, a waste of time that they should ever have lived. And he was afraid to die.

"What I fear is nothingness afterwards and death as an interruption of all I want to do, all I want to be. When I cling to the idea of eternity, the thought of my death becomes tolerable."

It was for the promise it made of life after death that he believed in religion. And it was because the roads, the bridges and all the other structures he was going to put up would last that he was going to become an engineer.

His mathematical mind could not understand the illogic of Desmond's death and he had seemed to be living with it as if it were his own or as if he had seen the seed of his own death in his friend's and been fascinated by it.

4

John smoked in the dark. The town which he could not see threw up to the sky the dim glow of its lights, and the thicker bush at the edge of the shelf which marked the beginning of the slope he had climbed up earlier was silhouetted against the glow.

The day after Stephen's funeral – by proxy for they had never discovered the body – he had pretended he was too sick to see Miriam who had come again to visit him. And in order to make up for his rudeness he went, the second Sunday after her visit, to her home. It was nearly two weeks since the incident on the beach and he had taken the decision to remove himself to the seclusion of the hill. In a way he come to take leave of her even though he did not say so.

She had just returned from Children's Mass and was having a cup of strong, black coffee to break her fast. Her pink hat which matched her dress and her purse were on a chair. They were sitting in the same front room where, with Stephen, they had sat the first time he visited her home. The window at which her father sat was opened. Miriam opened the other and the light poured into the room in broad beams on either side of the closed door. Particles of dust, showing many colours, hung in them.

"How's your mother?" he asked after he had settled.

"She's well," Miriam answered him. "She's in the back, in the kitchen."

The smell of grilled meat was in the air.

Miriam raised her voice and called to her mother. Fat, jolly Mrs Dezauzay came in briefly, shook his hand, asked about his mother. Then with a look at her husband which she believed furtive, said she was busy in the kitchen and went out again.

"And how are you?" he asked Miriam.

"Fine," she said.

"I'm sorry I was so sick when you came," he said.

"Glad you're well again. I hadn't seen you at the funeral and I wondered. That was all."

The smell of grilled meat seasoned with garlic was pleasant. And, with the quiet intervals of the conversation and the light, evocative. It was quiet, too, outside and through the open windows the sky was very blue and white soft clouds raced under it. The heat was already more than a memory he was beginning to feel of past Sunday mornings. He had walked through the heat and in the light but he had not observed either.

"How was the funeral?" he asked.

Miriam shrugged. "Funny," she said. "I knew it was only a covered piece of wood between the candles. It didn't mean anything. And it didn't make any sense at all."

Mrs Dezauzay came in with a tray. On plates on it there was meat, lettuce, tomatoes, bread and coffee. The smell of half-burnt garlic was very strong.

"Have a bite, John," Mrs Dezauzay said.

"It didn't mean anything," Miriam said, "and I wondered what I was doing there."

"What?" he asked. And then, "Oh, the funeral."

"Yes," Miriam said.

John took the tray from Mrs Dezauzay who was not listening to them and who, as soon as the tray was out of her hands, went across to where her husband was sitting before the window and did something to the collar of the fresh white shirt that he wore. With his eyes, John followed her. Suddenly, the tranquil brilliance he saw through the open window was the dazzling brilliance after the gloom behind the closed doors of the church. There was a sensation of abrupt heat, the sound of cocks crowing behind high walls, the emptiness of the streets and, above all, the hot quiet, like a pant. There was the firmness of light and shadow as he walked under the two-storeyed buildings with their clean, white fronts and their well-polished brass knockers; the bark of a dog jumping on the floor of the verandah over his head, the sight of a blue-and-white uniformed servant with a pram, the sight of a pink face as he went past, pink on white, the policemen marching down the centre of the hot street to change the guard. There was the wharf and the swimming boys, and their glistening, black, muscled bodies diving from the wharf's edge, from the quiet dipping stern of a berthed vessel or, sometimes, high up from a mast. Their bodies hung in the space between the mast and the sea, etched briefly against the blue of the sky and the white of the clouds beneath them.

He turned away from the window. The smell of grilled meat and half-burnt garlic was the smell of home on Sunday and of a time that seemed, now, a time of make-believe only. He had not been to Mass in years but it was only now at this precise moment of remembering that as if with a snap he had made a break. His memory had been like a gasp preceding it. Mrs Dezauzay had left the room. Miriam was looking at him.

"Have you come back?" she asked. She was smiling.

"Yes," he said, looking at her and smiling also. He began to eat. On the wall behind her the illuminated scroll which had been a gift to her father, after he had been the church organist for twenty-five years, hung under glass.

"Where have you been?" she asked.

"Far," he said, "very far."

Framed pictures of Miriam's father looked down upon him as he chewed the grilled, garlicked meat. There was one of him as a young man, very handsome with whiskers and carefully brushed mulatto hair. And there was the one with his wife on the day they were married.

"Somewhere I shall never go again," he said.

"I know the feeling," she said.

"Do you?"

He turned to the window again. The clouds fled silently in the bright light of the open. Framed against the window Mr Dezauzay's head was gaunt and the hair on it white and still aristocratic. The coffee was hot and very strong. He turned again to Miriam.

"Tell me," he said.

But she asked him a question instead.

"A place that was dear to you?" Her smile was faint and naughty. As if she were playing a parlour game.

"Yes," he said, "though I didn't know it at the time."

The piano was covered with pictures too. Most of them were pictures of the young man her father had been. John had the impression of a gay, almost carefree past.

"And not exactly a place either," he said.

"A time," it was no question and the way she said it was gay, like the clap of hands at a party.

He smiled that she was right.

"And now you feel you've lost it forever."

He nodded. Specks of dust danced colourfully in the broad beams of sunlight. They played over the old man's lap. His too-large trousers were tied with string. His brown hands, in the sunbeam, did not move.

John nodded.

"It happens." Beneath her plain statement John felt a hint or, as Miriam might have preferred to put it, a taint of personal sadness. Musically the church bells were calling the faithful out to High Mass.

"It's the feeling of Sunday morning as a child," he said, "after Mass."

"I know it," she said. There was a mixture of composure and excitement as she spoke. She was small, brown and pretty. He was smoking a cigarette now.

"Are you finished?" Mrs Dezauzay had come in again. She took the tray from him, tried not to appear to be watching her husband, smiled at John. She went out again.

"You'll never have it again," Miriam said.

"How do you know?" John asked.

"I know."

"Oh?"

"Once you've looked at something, really looked at it, then you've lost it."

Abruptly, John remembered the sensation his moment of memory had given him of a break with what it had evoked.

He said, "Perhaps you're right."

"A sort of loss of innocence," she smiled. Her serenity was like a wreath. Her pink dress and her smile the flowers that made it.

Suddenly, inexplicably, he envied her. He wished to see her as she had been when she came to his house the day Stephen had drowned, distraught and showing her pain. His wish surprised him. It was followed by another. He wished to see her sad and weeping, and dressed in black. He was ashamed to have such a wish. But it was insistent and his desire to see her unhappy and his shame at the thought were simultaneous.

He heard himself say, "You do look very well, you know."

"Eh?" He had taken her by surprise.

"You've recovered so completely."

"Recovered?" And then, "Oh."

Unable to stop he said, "I remember how you looked that evening when you came."

She was looking at him. He was smiling as he spoke. "You look so different now." It was as if he wanted to destroy Miriam for no other reason than because he had to.

"Your eyes," he said. "And your face as you listened."

She was looking at him, a hint of a smile on her face.

"You never said a word," he said, "not one. As if you hadn't heard anything I said to you."

"I didn't," she said.

He felt a prick of pleasure. He continued, at once eager and unwilling.

"Nothing?"

"No, not anything." His pleasure increased. He had led her back. Her serenity, under his guidance, would shed its leaves one by one.

"I remember the people outside. And that I had to wait for you to come from your room. I remember there was no light and I remember standing just inside the door in the dark and hearing the crowd talking outside."

He was happier.

"Then you came and struck the match and I saw light and shadow. But mostly I saw shadow."

"You didn't see me cry?"

The question which he had not meant to ask made him feel hypocritical. And yet to hear her say she had seen him cry would have attenuated his present feeling of disgust for his impotence to stop what he revelled in doing to her.

"Oh, yes. But only later. When I was in the street again. While

I was walking home I saw you and the round table between us and the painted calabashes that hung on the partition at your back. I am right? Those things are there?"

"Yes, they are there."

"And I hadn't been to your home before."

She was no longer smiling. But his feeling of satisfaction was going now. It was going as uncontrollably as it had come. And he was glad, as he had been sorry when it came, automatically. Then, abruptly, she shifted in her chair, took a deep breath and smiled again.

"That's past now," she said.

And his resentment came back and he heard himself say, "You're resilient," as if he wished to say with the completest accuracy that she was not.

"Am I?" she asked.

"Yes. You must know you are." He feared, even as he hoped it might be so, that his voice expressed resentment and, possibly, jealousy.

"I had no choice."

Mrs Dezauzay came in. She offered him some falernum she had made. Miriam also accepted a glass. Her mother did not offer her husband any. But she looked at him, pretending not to do so. Outside John heard footsteps as people were passing on their way to High Mass. The room was getting hotter. Mrs Dezauzay pulled the chair on which her husband sat away from the beam of sunlight. Only a small bit now played on his slippered feet. The rest, the spectrum of dust suspended in it, stretched from the window sill and lay on the wooden floor next to them.

"I had to forget," Miriam said.

"And have you?"

She looked at him. She was smiling without apparent malice. But he was smiling too and she could not see the malice which he resented but which, nevertheless, was behind the smile.

She said, "When I am not reminded."

And, again automatically, he heard himself say, "I am sorry."

She was quiet for some time. Then she said, "You told me the same thing that evening. I remember now. I hadn't remembered it before. How extraordinary."

It was, indeed, very strange. She had not remembered the one thing he told her that was true. And when he wished to hurt her, she was remembering it. It was not only strange but confusing as well. He heard the church bells, loud, unmusical, sending out an ultimate, staccato summons to the lingering faithful.

"What are you sorry for?" she asked.

"For reminding you again," he said.

He was sorry he could not explain to her, that she had forgotten the one sincere statement he had made, that she had lost Stephen, that he wanted so much and for no reason to hurt her, that her father was as he was, that finally, there was nothing whatever that he could do.

"Don't you think it is good sometimes to remember?" she asked.

"No." Not as he had been remembering lately.

"Oh, I do," she said. "Only, sometimes it seems impossible."

"I hadn't found so," he said.

"I have."

There was a pause.

Then she spoke. "When I left you that night I tried to remember Stephen and me and the things we had done and would never again do…"

Suddenly he found he did not want to hear about herself and Stephen. He interrupted, "You look well in pink."

"You're the only one who approves," she said. "I couldn't remember a thing."

He was thinking of what he could say to distract her.

"In the morning with my eyes still open I had a nightmare. I was in flat open country. I could smell flowers in the dark and could see them when I was away from them. I approached and each flower became a black burnt knob. But I could still smell the scent of flowers. It was terrible."

She smiled.

He felt no sympathy for her. He wished to say, "Good" to her.

He said, "I can imagine."

"So I awoke, dressed, and without any sleep at all, went to the church."

"God would help, of course. He always does."

"To Mass," she said, "not to God. It was the routine of habit I knew I had to submit to. And I went to work, without mourning, in uniform."

"The pink dress," he said.

"Yes," she said, "the pink dress. Mother does not approve of course."

"Do you know what it is like," she asked, "to feel empty?"

John smiled and did not answer.

"I wrapped Stephen and myself in emptiness for days," she said. "I shut out my mother and I shut out God. Then I was tired and gave up. I had been going to Mass and trying to understand. I still went to Mass but I stopped trying to understand."

John said nothing.

"I accepted."

John watched her. Outside a noise was advancing and increasing in volume. They heard the words MARY MUST COME BACK. And soon Old Alphonse, drunk already at eleven o'clock of that Sunday morning, passed before the house, his placard on his shoulder, and the words of his perpetual refrain written in red chalk upon it. Behind him, skipping, clapping their hands and chanting the words merrily aloud to the lame rhythm of the drunken shoemaker, the children followed.

It was as if Stephen's image had been a building on this approach of sound until it filled the whole of the small room with its presence. Neither the quick disappearance of the mob as it went past, nor the very gradual retreat of its sound had been able to remove the image afterwards. Alive, Stephen would certainly have followed the procession part way, from enjoyment and his own sense of the humorous, but also for whatever it could have afforded him for his future imitations of the shoemaker. Now Stephen would forever be linked with the drunkard in the memories of himself and of Miriam for whom his impersonations of Alphonse had so often provided entertainment.

Miriam and John looked at each other. Both smiled. It seemed all they could do. Stephen was only a memory which joined them now. And joined them each to Old Alphonse to whom they had never spoken.

"Do you think he really had a wife?" Miriam asked.

The memory they shared, that was Stephen, Miriam seemed determined to keep away.

"I don't know," he said. "Since I can remember, he has been waiting for Mary to come back."

Mrs Dezauzay came in.

"Was that Alphonse?" she asked.

"Yes, Mother," Miriam said. "Did he really have a wife?"

"I think so," Mrs Dezauzay said. She had looked at her husband already and was getting ready to get back into her kitchen. She was not really interested. "Any woman would leave him. He drinks too much."

"Did he though, for sure?" Miriam asked her.

"I don't know. He must have."

"Have you ever seen her?"

"No."

"Has anyone?"

Her mother looked once more at her husband who had been dismissed from his job for theft without gratuity or pension and whom she had never left. Nor ever would leave.

"Suppose he doesn't have any?" Miriam asked John.

"Never had any?" she laughed.

"Suppose it was just a joke he thought of one day long ago when he was drunk?"

"Or sober, perhaps," John said.

"And suppose," Miriam said, "it is no joke at all?"

"I wish I knew," John said.

"Me too."

Her father, who had not even stirred, was looking quietly out of his window.

5

In the dark, remembering, John smoked. The shapes of the
bushes he looked at were familiar. The night noises too. They had
bothered him at first. Now he was almost unaware of them. He
got up and walked to the edge of the shelf facing the town. Its
lights were far below him. Anne-Marie had been right. It was easy
to adjust. Disgustingly easy to adjust. Those lights, once, had
given him pleasure. Now he felt nothing, looking at them. He
turned away. He would go down to the old priest's house and play
chess. He thought of his torch. He did not bother to get it. He
knew all the tracks on this part of the hill. He had lived here long
enough for that.

Halfway down the path which led to where the old priest lived,
lower down the slope, he saw someone approaching with a
torchlight and for a moment thought it might be his friend. He
hoped it wasn't for his stock of rum was finished and he would
prefer to play at the old man's and drink some of the punch he
made so well. As the light came nearer and he, seeing the figure
of a woman, was about to step aside; he recognized Anne-Marie.

"What are you doing here?" he asked.

"Looking for you," she said out of breath. "I went to your
friend, the priest, but you weren't there. Would have saved me a
lot of this trouble."

She played the light of the torch on her shoes. They were wet
with the dew and a little muddy.

"You've forgotten," she said.

"Forgotten what?" he asked. "Not Harold's party?"

"Yes, Harold's party."

"Oh, he came? When did he come?"

"He arrived this morning."

PART TWO

6

"And so it was suicide."

Harold nodded.

"Suicide," John repeated.

And Stephen's cry, coming over to him on the wind, was no longer a cry inviting him to death and unfulfilment. Its echo rolled over him senselessly, with ugly deceit.

"I saw him," he said. "He was struggling. And he called out for help… It can't be true."

"But there's the letter," Harold said. "I've told you about it. Stephen wrote Derek that his father had used all his money. That he couldn't wait God knows how many years more. That he was going to kill himself."

"He might have planned it for some other time."

"Drown himself. He said he was going to drown himself."

"Surely he didn't have to drown himself when he was with me. He could have walked any other time to the beach to do so."

He was clinging to the security of his little world of self-blame as if he were afraid to leave it.

"Stephen wanted to live," he said.

He was afraid to leave his world and strike a new direction. It had been very real. It was impossible that it, too, should become dream. Suddenly he felt a deep resentment against Stephen for that which he was inflicting upon him. He would have now to advance in the dark, blindly, without knowing where he was going, nor why.

"I can't believe it," he said. "I won't believe it."

He was not going to be the plaything of his dead friend to be tossed, like flotsam or his own body, on the waves.

"We received the letter late," Harold was saying. "Derek was about to answer when Anne-Marie's telegram came. 'Stephen drowned. Accident.'"

"Accident." John looked at the word.

Accident or design, nothing had changed. Everything was, eternally, the same. Would be, forever, part of him. He had not moved. He had stood, afraid, and had not moved. That was, that is, that would always be. Its omnipresence was like God's. He would never be able to escape its implacable eye. And he felt the need to expose what it saw as if to lessen the intensity of its gaze or as if that which was in him, and was dirty and undesirable, might be cleaned by Harold's looking at it.

"How could no one have known?" Harold asked.

"How could anyone have known?"

"Not even suspect?"

"Not even suspect."

Stephen's unseen face in the dark of their walk that evening he was kicking the stone he could not see. But he heard the voice. "Maybe I can swim, eh?" Could Stephen have been planning suicide even then? He remembered Stephen's reaction to Desmond's death. He was not sure what was and what was not. And he was resenting his dead friend more and more. His resentment grew at the same rate as his desire to show himself to Harold.

"Perhaps I might have saved him, Harold," he said, "but I didn't try."

He waited.

Harold said nothing.

"You're not surprised?" John asked.

"I'm not surprised, no. Why should I be?"

John found himself thinking that perhaps Harold was not the right person to confess to. Harold had always tended to put himself first. This thought was involuntary. He had expected, almost desired, Harold to react and Harold had not. And yet at the same time that he wanted to show his cowardice to Harold, for Harold to comment on, he wished also to attenuate it. His desire to expose himself and, at the same time, protect himself from too much exposure was instinctive and involuntary.

He said, "He was too far out for me to get to him. But I didn't try."

He believed now, after what Harold told him, that Stephen was too far. And yet it was possible that Stephen had not been too far. He was confused.

"I am a coward," he said, "you understand?"

Harold said nothing.

"Don't you say anything?" It was as if he were disappointed.

"How can it matter that you didn't try?" Harold asked.

"Ah, but that's what matters, nothing else. Don't you see?"

"And afterwards I went to the police and lied. I lied to his mother and I lied to Miriam."

Her broken face was framed in the drawing-room of his mind. It stood out from the other images there as if at the end of a projection. His pity for her and his self-disgust were the huge screen on which her image was projected.

"Poor girl," he thought.

He would have liked to wrap her in the vastness of his pity and of his shame.

"Poor girl," he said.

And he felt resentment against Stephen not only for what he had done to him but also for what he had done to her.

"His mother…" Harold began.

John hadn't thought of Teacher Amy. Yet her loss had been no less than Miriam's. Once death had been kind to her. When Son died she had been mentioned in the papers, received in Government House, honoured and fêted. Her status had bloomed as if it thrived on his flesh decomposing somewhere in Germany. She had been like a woman fulfilled and she had worn her mourning as another might have worn a smile. But the war had ended and the island forgot, and it had been on Stephen that the need of the retired village headmistress had depended for its nourishment. Death, no longer kind, had waited until the very last minute to cheat her. She would never have a son again. But Miriam was young. And John was young. In the fight Teacher Amy had waged with Miriam for Stephen he had always been on Miriam's side. And now it was Miriam who was at once the symbol, for him, of Stephen's hurt and, also, the receptacle for the pity which enabled him to rise above the resentment that hurt made him feel.

He reflected that he had never felt sorry for Stephen that he was dead or that his plans, with his death, had come to an end. He had been angry with himself, and with Stephen for making him angry. He had been shocked. His pride in himself had been hurt. Stephen had only been an instrument for him. He wished to show this also to Harold.

He said, "Stephen's death never touched me. I have never felt sorry for him. And Stephen was my best friend."

Who committed suicide and took you to see it. The thought was immediate.

And he was resentful again remembering what Stephen had introduced him to on the beach that day.

"I felt shame," he said, "and regret for what his death showed me of myself."

He looked at Harold.

"I wonder if you understand?" he asked. "I can never be sure now what I'll do the next minute, tomorrow or the day after."

"Look, John," Harold began to say, "all this sitting and thinking…"

"Because I'm afraid," John interrupted. "To sit and think is safe. Otherwise it would be for me, like living with a guard always at my side. As if I were a madman and there was no place to put me in."

"But you can't solve anything here."

"I can solve it nowhere else."

"I would have liked to be sorry for Stephen. I knew that if I could I would feel much better. Only, once I knew that, sorrow was impossible. It was like buying peace with old coins or dirty notes. Like paying ransom with counterfeit money."

He took out a cigarette now and smoked.

"You know," he said, "people are hell?"

And he continued, "I'd go out and everywhere people would be sympathetic. That irritated me. They knew nothing and they dared to sympathize. I was dying to tell them what had really happened on that beach if only so they could leave me alone." He snorted, "But the courage, I didn't have the courage. So I remained at home. I avoided them. It was easier to do that."

"And then, at home, my mother made me feel like a stone

around her neck. She, too, did not know. And she, too, dared to be sympathetic."

"Your mother? She might even have known and be sympathetic."

"I think," John said, "then I should have despised her."

"I should have despised her," he repeated softly, "even more than I despised myself."

It was as if his mother had known and had been sympathetic. He was in his home again in her bedroom and his mother's ill and implacable eye smothered him quietly with its sympathetic concern.

"Let's get the hell out of here, Harold. I want a drink."

They drove in Harold's hired car down the hill, through the town, and emerged from it on the road that led past the Gardens to the beach. They came to the club on the sea's edge. On one of the two tennis courts Anne-Marie was playing. John and Harold went upstairs and Harold ordered drinks. They sat on the verandah facing the sea. The sound of its small waves was hardly audible.

During the twenty-minute ride, while Harold drove, John had sat next to him, smoking his cigarette and looking out of the window of the car. And because he had been thinking of his mother he was, suddenly, coming home from college again and there was the ring of people standing in front of the small shop she had opened near the wharf. His mother was standing in the doorway of the small shop, alone. It seemed she was about to cry. He went to her side; she might not have seen him. She was looking at Chou Macaque. Chou was standing in the middle of the ring of onlookers and was inviting his mother to come down on the pavement. She stood in the doorway. She would not go down to the pavement: she would neither retreat to the back of the small shop. Chou's imprecations rolled out of his black lips into the hot air, dirty as the clothes he wore, uglier than his unshaved face with gaps where the batons of policemen had knocked his teeth out, as deformed, in his mixture of patois and English, as his flat bare feet, cracked between the toes and at the heels, and black in the cracks with dirt. She stood without a word in the doorway and he could hear her heavy breathing behind her balled-up, cornered-rat's resistance. He had gone cold with anger even as he bristled to protect her. And he was ashamed, too, despite his anger. For he was afraid of the giant standing on the pavement. His feeling of inadequacy was increased as he listened to the sympathetic murmuring of the crowd, made up almost only of women, and realized that not one of them had come to her aid. It was the feeling that all that could be provided for her at that moment was this oral, almost mechanically-lipped sympathy, and nothing else, that had reduced him. Chou Macaque, with his oaths and threats, was a priest and they were the chorus giving their responses to him.

Later, under the heat from the galvanized roof of the shop, sitting before the steaming plate of rice and fish that was to have been lunch, he had cried with unexploded rage, quietly, and with helplessness. And as he saw her quickly calm again, the ball of her resistance unwound now, he felt the first conscious feelings of resentment for the way she had chosen. As if she might have remained safely at home, in the drawing-room, with the cat and the knitting. She had unwound herself so easily that it must have been something she had become accustomed to from long habit. And looking at her as if he had just discovered who she was, and under the shock of his discovery, he despised her for accepting all so meekly and himself for being the cause of it.

He sat gazing out of the car and to think of his father after the memory of that incident had not been difficult. For in many ways much of his attitude had been conditioned by the help he imagined, from observing the parents of his friends, his father could have given to his mother. It had been very easy from there, and without any understanding whatsoever of his parents' relationship, to apportion blame. The early memory, which was not necessarily of something that actually took place, and his father's strange voice saying, "You too proud, Lena, your pride will kill you," he had not forgotten. And at his mother's funeral he had seen his father crying. But his memories of his father were mostly brutal and unpleasant and, after their last meeting, he knew that forever his parents would be a closed book to him.

He had been surprised to see his father standing outside of his room in the barracks waiting for him. They had not spoken for years. After they had fought he had put his father out of his mind because to deny existence was easier than to hate and because, in time, to dwell on what might have been was more tiresome than to accept what was. His father must surely have visited the house several times but it was only two incidents he remembered clearly now.

It was Thalia's laughter while he stood, his back to her, and pissed against the wooden fence of the yard, that he had been listening to. And when he had no longer heard it, he had turned to see her disappearing behind the corner of his mother's house, her hand to her mouth, and, at the same time, felt himself lifted by one hand and the heavy repeated stings of the thick black belt his father had removed from his waist. He was only eleven years old then but the memory of this must have helped to provoke his adolescent resentment and the expression he gave to it a few years later. More than the pain of the strap it had been the feeling of being unjustly punished by someone who, now, no longer had the right to punish, that had moved him.

After the first lash had stung his back therefore he hit his father in the face with all the power behind his fifteen-year-old fist (he was already as tall as his father), hit him again with his resentment and his exasperation, and hit him once more, in a sudden, uncontrolled rage, sobbing now, but without pain and with the relief his actions afforded him.

He had been surprised to pick himself up from the floor, so sudden had been the calm fury of his father, the blood dripping from his mouth where the big fist had hit it, neither of them saying anything.

He could have killed his father very easily then. There was this look of undethronable authority on his father's face that would have driven his growing feeling of helplessness to murder if it were possible. And his father's calm figure standing stockily on its slightly parted legs, looking at him with considering detachment as if he were some strange animal, no surprise on its face, and slowly putting back the belt into the tabs at its trousers' waist, seemed to mock his inadequacy.

He had stood there waiting to establish as strongly as possible the point of his defiance, hating more and more the smug and distasteful self-assurance of the powerful man in front of him.

His father's visit had been the first attempt on either side to break the silence this incident had caused.

That was why he had been so surprised when he emerged from the little English cemetery to see his father waiting outside of his room for him. He had been even more surprised to see that the image his father had always been for him was not that of his father now. The smooth bullishness had given place to a sagging of the cheeks on either side of the face which looked flat; and the once fleshed neck and its suggestion of great strength which he had so hated to look at, contained hollows now and loose flesh. He reflected with a sort of distant wonder that, during his mother's illness when, occasionally, his father had come to see her, he had not noticed these changes at all. He had not even bothered to look at him.

"Good evening," he said. "I hope you've not been waiting very long."

"No. Not very long," his father said.

"I went for a walk," John said. "If I'd known…"

"It's all right," the brown arm in short sleeves made a gesture.

"You're perspiring," John said, "did you walk?"

"No. But I didn't know exactly where you were. I had to look."

"I'm sorry," John said.

"I came about your mother's house," his father said.

John said nothing.

"Somebody wants to buy it," his father said.

"You may sell it."

"What about the things in it?"

"You can sell them too."

"Everything? The bed, the tables? Your books?"

"Yes, sell everything. I don't need them."

"The wardrobe is very good," his father said, "it would be difficult to get one like it now."

"Sell everything," John said. "You may take the wardrobe if you like."

"I don't want it. I have my own. But you may need it later on."

"Sell it then."

"All right," Mr Lestrade said. "I'll sell it and give you the money."

"I don't want it."

"Eh?"

"I don't want the money."

"Listen to me," Mr Lestrade said, "the things are yours. They are not mine."

John said nothing.

"If I sell them you must take the money."

John did not answer at once. Not so long ago his father had bought a car which, because he had learnt so late to drive, he drove with caution and with difficulty. The image of his father sitting awkwardly behind the steering wheel of his second-hand car made him smile. And he felt better.

"I don't want the money," he said and then maliciously, "maybe you can use it for something."

"The money is yours."

"I'm sure you can find something to do with it," smiling insolently.

He noticed that the veins on the sides of his father's neck were swollen. His father's face had ceased to be brown. It was red now. That pleased him.

"I cannot keep it," his father said. "In that case perhaps I should not sell it."

"Perhaps," nonchalantly, "but I don't care. Do as you wish."

His father, angry, was trying to control himself.

"I am only trying to help," he said.

Too late, John had thought, much too late. He was angry.

"I did not ask for it," he said.

"You don't have to be rude. And I don't have to stand your rudeness."

Hit, John thought, hit me now.

But he stopped smiling and said, "I'm sorry."

The older man said nothing but John saw his face soften a bit at this unusual apology.

He said, "I agreed you should sell the house."

"I won't sell it unless you accept the money."

John shrugged his shoulders. The dark had fallen. His father slapped a bare arm.

"Shall we go inside?"

They went inside. He lit the lantern, gave his father the chair and sat on the edge of the cot.

"I can put the money into your account," his father said, "if you have one."

"I don't want you to do that."

This man eager to help was beginning to worry him.

"You're just as stubborn as your mother."

The remark surprised John. He looked his father in the face. The forehead, thrusting out from behind the receding line of the close-cut hair, was as aggressive as ever.

"Must I give you the keys then?"

"I don't want them. But you may do as you like."

His father's skin was almost yellow in the light of the lantern. Just as he had felt on the beach with Rose, John had the sensation that he was dreaming and that, soon, he would awake. The room, closed against the insects, was becoming hot. His father got up to leave. From beneath the out-thrust brows, his eyes, out of the yellow face, looked at the young man. The face he looked at, but for the colour of the skin and its youth, might almost have been a replica of his own. From his own face John's eyes looked back. Their attitudes resumed those of their last meeting when they had fought. Between them reconciliation was not possible.

But, already too, his father was ceasing to be the man he had always, until then, been for him. His father went away and still irritated John had gone down the path that led to the old priest's home.

The road Harold drove on, following the line of the shore, was empty and there were only coconut trees on the sides of it.

There were so many things about his mother and his father he would have liked to know. There was so much to understand. And it had been so easy not to understand and, not understanding, take up set positions.

The car was moving at a good pace over the empty twisting road. Beyond the coconuts on the left there was the sea lying blue and flat. You could not tell what was going on beneath its flat surface. He had been many times with his mother to the beach.

And suddenly, not far now from the club, John began to laugh.

He laughed so much that Harold had to ask what he was laughing at.

"I just remembered," John said, laughing still.

"Must be very funny," Harold said unsmiling.

"It's about my mother," John said.

"The one you would have despised?" Harold's voice lifted quietly, like an eyebrow.

"The very one," still laughing.

As if there could have been another.

Harold did not understand. John was laughing loudly in the car.

"You can't miss any more school, John," his mother said. "Wear my shoes."

"The boys will laugh at me."

"You have to go to school. Take them."

"The boys will laugh at me, Ma."

"Try them. They not bad."

"Let me go for mine from the shoemaker, please."

"I must pay him first. And I don't have money now. He won't give them."

"They won't fit. They too big."

"Try them let me see."

"They too big Ma. Look how big they are." He held them up.

"Try them. It getting late, John. Put them let me see."

"Ma, the boys going to laugh, Ma."

"Don't mind the boys. You have to go to school."

They were too big but only just.

She said, "Very nice. You see? A piece of cloth for the toes."

The black strap which buttoned across his instep seemed the symbol of girlishness. He began to cry. His mother came back with a piece of cloth.

"Stop crying, John," she said, "a big boy like you. What you crying for?"

She was stuffing cloth into the tips of the shoes.

"Try them now."

He put the stuffed shoes on. His toes were not comfortable against the cloth.

She took the shoes and removed some of the cloth. "You not shame?" she asked him, "crying like that for nothing?"

"I'll get your shoes tomorrow," she said, "stop crying now."

The shoes fitted.

He was crying.

He had had to wear them for a week.

John was still laughing when Harold turned into the stony path leading to the club. They sat over their drinks on the verandah watching the small waves run up and break upon the shore. They did not speak much. Harold mentioned briefly his plans. They were the same as John's would have been. Except that Harold was more determined, more driving and, certainly, unless he had changed, would push them to the utmost success. John felt calm and a little sad. His sadness was as quiet as the light itself, now that the sun had gone down, and as soothing as the murmuring of the small waves. He felt as fluid as they. An absence of tension, a suppleness of spirit, the sensation of not being here on the verandah listening to Harold discussing his possibilities, although he knew he was, made him feel light, etherealized, the expression, the very symbol of peace. And, listening to Harold, freedom.

Anne-Marie and Miriam appeared.

"Hi."

"Hello."

"Still drinking?" Anne-Marie asked.

"It was a good party last night," Harold said. "Thanks."

Under her short skirt Anne-Marie's legs were long and very shapely.

"Buy you a drink," Harold said, "both of you."

"Beer for me please," Anne-Marie said. She was wet. And very beautiful, John thought. He would not look at Miriam.

"And you Miriam?" Harold asked.

"Rum punch."

Harold was getting up. Anne-Marie stopped him.

"We'll have them at the counter," she said, "I'll tell Charlie to put it on your bill."

The girls went inside.

"Two fine women," Harold said.

"Yes they are."

"And still unmarried. It's a shame."

"Not their fault, is it?"

"No."

"Anne-Marie's not interested."

"Pity. She must be nearly twenty-seven or -eight."

"Yeah. Derek's friend, really, more than ours."

"Derek made a mistake."

"Oh, he knows. Sheila's all right. But not Derek's speed. Nor Anne-Marie's class."

"It's not easy to be in Anne-Marie's class."

"True. Took me a long time, though, to find out. Remember how often we quarrelled?"

"The only man you never quarrelled with was Derek."

"Is that so?"

"Is that so?" John mimicked him. "It's things like that you used to say in your phony B.B.C. accent. It's remarkable though. You've lost it."

"I guess I was a bit of a prig," Harold admitted.

"A bit?"

"Well?"

"You always knew more than everybody else. Were always more correct than anybody else. Except Derek. And that was only because he was older."

"Well, wasn't I right most times?" Harold laughed. "However did the group stand me?"

"Well, it was your father's house we were using, wasn't it? And your father's cash. Besides Mr Montague left us pretty much alone."

"The Old Man left us alone all right."

"You haven't changed, have you?"

"You know who was at the airport to meet me, even though you weren't?"

"Who?"

"Dédé."

"She must have been very pleased to see you. Dédé was the only one you got along with."

" 'Eh, eh. Mistah Harold.' And she began to feel me as though she were blind and wanted to be sure it was me. 'Mais gardé-i 'on.' And she began to laugh and to cry and to hug me. 'But look at him, 'on,' she repeated. Then 'my child, my child.' As if I were really her child."

The girls came out onto the verandah to say they were leaving. Anne-Marie waved a carefree arm. She was wearing a sweater now.

"Goodbye, Miriam," John said.

"I hope that Miriam doesn't do like Anne-Marie," Harold said. John said nothing.

Harold said, "I couldn't tell whether Anne-Marie was glad or not that Derek couldn't come as he had planned to."

"I think that's what she wants. To keep everybody guessing."

"I don't think Derek can come for months. Perhaps not for a year."

"Mrs Charles must have been very disappointed."

"She was. But you know her. She tried not to show it. She was glad to see me and hear what I had to say about Derek, Sheila and the children. Then I told her about Sheila's illness. How serious it had been and that Derek had to change his mind. Took it quite well though."

"She's a giant among mothers," John said.

"You're the authority on them," Harold said.

"You know, you really haven't changed at all?"

"At least I can say this for the Old Man," Harold said, "he gives Dédé an allowance monthly. She's too old now to work."

"Mr Montague is a very kind and friendly man," John said. "He has always been."

"To my friends perhaps."

"To anyone who would leave him alone."

"Why should I?"

"It's too damn easy to blame other people," John said.

"Maybe. But nobody can defend him."

"What has he done anyhow?"

"It's not what he does. But how he does it. He must remember that I have to live and work here."

"Leave him alone," John said.

Then he thought, it's so easy to give advice. And he decided to stop. Harold, he decided, had not changed. And suddenly he wondered whether, to others, he had seemed to have changed.

And how much. And he thought again of the days when they were in Harold's home over his father's grocery and rum-shop combined. The plans they had often made there had turned out very differently. He remembered Mr Montague's courtesy to Harold's friends and his pleasure when they came to the house. He himself had never seemed to be there. He was either downstairs in the business or, at night when it was closed, out at whatever he was doing in the town. Many nights from Harold's room, Derek, Stephen, Harold and John would hear the slam of the door, the soft tread on the stairs. And, on Saturdays, when he entertained his friends in the rum-shop after closing hours, for he never took them to the apartment above because his son disliked him to do so, they heard voices and laughter well into the night. The old merchant who had worked his way from scratch would then drop his restrained courtesy, reserved for the friends of his son, and his loud voice and his laughter came to them upstairs, with that of his friends, while they planned. But those plans had turned out very differently indeed.

And he thought of their parents. His mother was dead. Teacher Amy, still alive, and with none of her two sons left, unfulfilled. Old Dezauzay looked out of his window. Even Mrs Charles, alive, too, and hoping to see her son, had had to postpone her pleasure. Nothing, before the event, was sure. Only after, the action performed, the wheel stopped firmly at the base of the hill. One went slowly, a step at a time; or one went quickly, in a headlong dash. And no one knew what was around the corner. Any plan must seem illogical; and hope, in the phrase of the island, only a motorboat.

"Hope is a moto'-boat," he said aloud.

"What's that?"

He had once seen a woman drumming for the masqueraders on New Year's day, her eyes closed, her hands moving feverishly, unaware of everything around her, even the dancers she played for. She had seemed asleep. And her drumming must have been her dream. And Amélie had walked from cross to cross, her lips moving feverishly, her eyes closed. She too had seemed asleep.

"Hope. It's a moto'-boat."

"What are you talking about?"

"Illusion and reality."

"You must be mad."

"Amen."

"You've been sitting on your arse for too long," Harold said.

"And I will continue."

"To do what? To sit?"

"And wait."

"For what?"

"I don't know. Maybe for what I thought I was. Or what I want to be. And don't ask me what it is either because I don't know. It'll have to be different that's all."

"Different? From what?"

"From what I discovered on the beach."

"And you'll wait. For how long?"

"I don't know. I have to wait, that's all."

"And in the meantime?"

"I have to sit and wait," John said, "that's all I know."

"You've been waiting a long time."

"Yes. And I'll wait some more."

"What are you waiting for?"

"I told you not to ask. I don't know."

"You're not getting any younger, you know that?"

"Yup."

"And you have to live. You need money for that. And you can't get it from sitting on your behind."

"Yup," John said gaily. "Right again. And we've discussed this several times before. You, Derek, Stephen and I."

"But now," he added after a pause, "I can only sit and wait."

He had often sat and watched the acceptance, by young men and women, of their life on the island, their mediocre, as it seemed to him, empty life. He had ceased to be sure whether the contempt he had felt for them was born of their acceptance or of his inability to be like them. It had seemed clear to himself and Stephen that, this side of professionalism and money, life on this drifting ship of an island could not ever be worthwhile. Now he was not sure that, for him, the other side, the side that now Harold was on, could be either. Reacting, he had been preoccupied with the money and the prestige a profession could acquire for him on the island. It was Stephen who had wished, literally and meta-phorically, to carve his life out of stone. John had been about to trace his in sand only; a wave, a casual gust of wind would have effaced it forever. As it would efface Harold's in time. As it had effaced those of all the lawyers and doctors, and those of the policemen and the labourers he had ever known.

And it was Stephen who had died. And who, perhaps, had been right.

The noises of the sea increased. The waves were beginning to run higher up the slope of sand. Perceptibly it was getting darker. Harold went inside for more drinks.

During those five years, John thought, he had been like a somnambulist waiting to awake. Nothing he did then had any significance, except the pain of his waiting. For the pain, like his somnambulist state, was transitory. It could only last so long as he had not awakened. His love during that time, with its promise of permanence, he had repudiated. And of the imper-manent, dreamlike actions he had performed, like a man filling his void on the toilet-seat with a cigarette or a newspaper he had already read, the memory of not even a single one gave him pleasure or satisfaction now. Nor had it then, once the action had been performed. And that was why his affairs had been so many. He had skipped from one to the other, desperately, afraid to raise his head and look at the emptiness that would confront him. He had been like the drumming woman. And her drum-ming had perhaps been to her what his affairs, his drinking, his chess, his job in the Service he had never taken seriously, and the friendships which he had used like cloaks had been, all of them, to him.

With Stephen it had been otherwise. The future had belonged to him and he had already begun to live it out. Miriam had been the symbol of the solidity of his belief. Yet he had wanted to commit suicide. Very probably he had done so. John did not understand. No longer even wished to understand. Stephen's death, now, had another, more special, relevance. After it, the aspirations, the ambitions, the determination for achievement, in the island's context, which had sharpened the point of his pain while he waited and, like the pain itself, had been very real, became a dream. His remorse, his anguish, had become the only reality. Now it, too, was becoming dream in its turn. He was aware of the impermanence of things. All was illusion and, finally, consolatory only. And glimpsing this, he could no longer have the pressing need for self-fulfilment, social and financial, that had been driving him so unremittingly before it. As he had said to Harold, who was returning now with the drinks, he could only wait and see.

The lights of the club came on, suddenly, shutting out all that was outside their radius. The sea was now only the sound of itself breaking and running up the sand. Gradually his eyes became accustomed again and he could see the white luminous crests of the waves as they broke beyond the area of light, and, in the distance behind them, the flat darkness of the sea. He could also feel the sandflies which had come out now and were stinging his ankles and his bare arms. Harold ordered supper and they ate steak, canned peas, salad and fried potatoes. At one stage Harold mentioned that he had met Rose in England. Rose felt like a very very long time ago.

But John still remembered the very pleasant girl that she had been.

7

He discovered, however, that he could not sit and wait for very long. Harold's revelation had initiated an end. He thought less and less of his mother, Stephen and the past few months ceased gradually to intrude, and he found himself looking forward again. The phrase which had stopped at the series of dots began to stretch itself out again in little desires, confused, imprecise; and the impatience with his existence on the island began again to make itself felt. Vague stirrings of the spirit made his life uncomfortable. They were like the itch on his body of a skin he was in the process of discarding.

He began to plan again, vaguely and without knowing what it was he was planning for. His inactivity began again to weigh upon him and the feeling of dissatisfaction he used to experience before Stephen's death began again to make him squirm and be restless. Stealthily, the urge to act, to give point and meaning to his existence, insinuated itself, made him uncomfortable like something placed in his bed to prevent him from falling asleep again. He was propelled by his desire; but he was propelled now towards no definite goal. He was like a sail filled to bursting with wind and moving over an open sea, no land in sight, without a compass, without direction of any kind.

"I feel like a piece of wood," he said once to his friend, the ex-minister, "a very small piece of wood drifting on a wide sea."

"Drift then," the old man had replied, knowing that no piece of wood, no matter how small, could go on drifting, even on the widest of oceans, forever. "Somewhere at the end of your drifting, sometime, there will be land."

He had been fighting despair and teaching hope to the members of his various parishes for so long now that it had become habit for him to do so. Recently he had been teaching it to himself.

"Drift, John," he said, "with hope and with patience and with faith." Then aware that he was sounding like the priest he had ceased to be, and anxious to correct himself before John and his professed unbelief in God, he added, "If one loses faith in oneself, then all is lost."

"But you're old," John said, "and waiting to die. To drift towards death must not be very difficult."

"For some, yes, it is not," the old minister smiled.

John remembered his mother and her struggle against death. "And for you?" he asked.

"For me it is not difficult."

It was not difficult because he was resigned. It was easy for the old to become resigned.

"I am young though," John said, "and I want to live. And to do. Sometimes it is as if my hands were tied and all around there was possibility and achievement if only I could free my hands to grasp them."

"I thought you said you were not interested in achievement." The old priest was smiling mischievously.

"And I'm not," John said, "not any more. Not in achievement as they know it here."

"And where do they know the achievement you're looking for?" the ex-priest asked.

John smiled at his friend's bantering tone. They were in the minister's house on the lower slope of the hill on which the barracks were. They had stopped playing chess and were drinking rum-punch which the old minister liked and which he had learnt to make very well. Ever since they had met each other in the military cemetery near the barracks and had discovered that they had at least chess in common they had become friends. The old man, amateur historian, taught John, in the intervals between chess which he enjoyed but played badly, and over several glasses of punch which he enjoyed and drank well, more of the history of the West Indies and of his own island than John had learnt in all his years at school. It was the ex-priest who made it so clear to him that less than a hundred years ago his ancestors, the black ones, were slaves, and his ancestors, the white ones, were their masters. The Abolition of Slavery had always been for him, up to that time, a phrase only. It was the old man who made him feel that he was a part of that phrase. John was very fond of him.

"I don't know," John smiled back at his friend.

"And what is the achievement you're looking for?"

"I don't know either, it seems."

"Surely you must?"

"I know more what it isn't than what it is."

"And what isn't it?"

"I'm no longer looking for suburban hill houses or respectability."

"Respectability? Are you going to give that up? Here?" The old man was poking fun. "You wouldn't survive," he said. "You must have two things here. Respectability. Or money. Or both."

His eyes twinkled. His big head seemed to press down on the thick short neck with the folds in it. He was enjoying himself. But only outwardly. He was very concerned about John.

"I was going to say that the other thing I was not looking for was money."

"That's what you need most," the old priest said, "lots of it."

"Or," he added, "you can become a priest."

They sat without talking for some time.

"You must wait, John," the old man said then.

It was the very same thing John had himself told Harold. Already he was finding it exhausting to wait.

"I feel I have waited for so long," he said.

The old man said nothing. Once in one of the many rectories he had used like hotels, he had forgotten which one, he had awakened during the night with a pain in the stomach and had had to go rather urgently to the lavatory, the way to which he dimly remembered from the directions his host had given him earlier on when he had arrived. He had turned on the light which was just within the door and had hurriedly gone and sat down on the bowl, his head in his hands. After the first relief he had looked up. An old man his pyjamas hanging about his knees, his face haggard and discomposed, the black hairs springing out of the hollow over the distended abdomen, was looking steadily at him. He had

94

thought later that, for his parishioners, to remind them of their mortality, a mirror in the lavatory might be a good thing. But not, certainly, for ministers who carried their knowledge always with them to share with the members of their parishes. But he had had his shock. An entire lifetime. He had spent an entire lifetime waiting. And he was still waiting. The satisfaction still had not yet come. His ministry, certainly, had not given it to him. He had found no satisfaction in converting a semi-pagan people to the externals only of a religion which he offered without explanation or teaching. And under the circumstances he could not do otherwise. The bickering and quarrelling among the sects, for whom the people seemed less souls to be saved than cows to be branded, or slaves to be marked, disgusted him. Catholics and Protestants had seemed to be buying on the open market and he had no urge to take part in the huge auction. His work, then, had given him very little satisfaction indeed. In fact it had steadily decreased as he had continued to work. The New Religion had been only another form of superstition. The people used it to find lost objects, obtain favours and promotion in their work, to spite their enemies. And they used it because, like the beach, it was there. For many it was an opportunity to put away the drab clothes of the week and dress. And for many others it was an opportunity to put away the drab clothes of their lives and hope.

He said, "There's nothing else, John, and you must wait some more."

In the end he had resigned from his ministry and become a teacher. To teach Charity and Love and the humbling awareness that all were children in the sight of God. And after several years the satisfaction he had been led to expect when he left Australia for these islands still had not arrived. As John said, he was old now and there could not be, or should not be, much more that he could be waiting for.

He looked at his young friend and he felt that, if only he could help to guide him out of the tunnel he stood in, then waiting for so long might not have been entirely in vain.

8

As the old man had said to John that day there was nothing else to do but wait. And while he waited he fell into his old habits again. Saturday nights he went to the clubs, each one in turn, until near dawn, he left the last one, very drunk, tired and cursing himself as he walked past the figures of shawled women on their way to early Catholic Mass. While the bells of the cathedral rang out the Angelus, he walked wearily up the hill mumbling to himself, ridiculing the shadowy figures and their faith, drunk and alone, and still unsatisfied. The whole sea of possibility stretched before him and the wind of his urge filled him and pushed him blindly. He was like a Greek god, dispossessed and powerful, choked with the power and authority he could not make use of.

One Saturday, at two in the morning, he found himself outside the *Stick*. He knew he had been drinking with some "friends" and remembered that he had driven down from the *Sea Blue* when it had closed. But his "friends" had left him and he could not remember where. He did not care. He wanted to push his drinking and the temporary pleasure it afforded him to the utmost limits. He would have pushed those limits even farther back if he could in order to prolong the night, to deny existence to time and duration, to transform them into an infinity of space in the middle of which he could run, as on a treadmill, in an unceasing effort that led to nowhere. He wanted to consume himself in one continual, inebriated effort until he dropped, from exhaustion, into a state which, in the completeness with which it would efface everything, would be analogous to the state of death. He stood in the middle of the road where the car had dropped him as if uncertain in which direction he should make the first step, his head down, never still, his hands along his sides, swaying forward to the very tips of his toes and then backwards onto his heels until he had to step back to prevent the fall; then stepped forward again to the very spot where he had been standing. Inside the club, the orchestra blared out its music inharmoniously, in clumsy imitation of the American recording its members had learnt it from. He made a gesture of distaste.

"Imitation," he mumbled, standing unsteadily, "always and everywhere imitation, now and forever, amen. A race of imitators. The best bloody imitators in the whole world. The most inept, too."

He raised his head and it fell again on his chest.

"Cows. Big, fat, ugly cows. Black cows. Brown cows. Yellow cows. Brown, black and yellow cows. Chewing the cud of other cultures, other habits, other religions. Other everything."

The music irritated him more.

"Bullshit."

Brief flashes of speech, very English, very much admired, passed before his muddled mind's disdain. Awkward, black figures in zoot suits, returned from the orange fields of Florida, walked ignorantly through the night of his thinking.

"Clowns."

He began to move, at last, towards the club.

"Clowns."

He stood again.

Black-robed, woollen-suited figures walked solemnly, wiping their perspiring faces with white handkerchiefs. The thin line of the collars of their shirts was very white between the blackness of their faces and that of their suits and robes.

"Clowns."

He began to walk again.

"Bloody clowns. All of us."

His smile was like a grimace.

"We outclowned them at cricket, though. The ape out-aped. Poetic justice."

He was stumbling now over the path of stones that led to the door. He himself was one of the clowns, a harlequin wearing uneasily the striped clothes that were his symbol.

"Bastards."

He struck a stone with his foot and nearly fell but he stuck out his hand and, luckily, it came in contact with the wall. He stood for a while after this near disaster.

"Fuck everything," he shouted, "fuck every fucking thing."

The music covered the sound of his words.

"Fuck every fucking thing," he repeated, mumbling the words. "Why the hell should I care?"

He said it like someone who cares and, caring, pretends he does not. He pushed open the door and stood blinking into the very bright light of the room. The music was very, very loud and very, very irritating.

At least there was the rum, thank God.

He made his way to the bar. He had to push to get to the counter, to shout to make himself heard. Then, his drink in his hand, and automatically better, he moved away from the counter. He stood in the heat of the crowded room, the smell of sweat all around him and, suddenly, he felt very alone and that here was not the place for him. He had reached the very limit of his drinking. He forced himself to drink like a patient taking medicine he abhorred but that he knew was good for him. He was tired. He was dissatisfied. He was alone. Briefly, from the confusion of dancers, the tall figure of a woman showed. Her teeth flashed out of her black face. Her thighs were strong against the too-tight dress. She was gone, swallowed up again by the sea of dancers, but he could follow the bobbing of her floating head. It drifted into the centre then came out again to the edge where he could see all of her splendid figure. He could feel the uncontrolled rising of his lust.

They danced the next number. Holding her, he felt the muscles of her back as she moved.

"You new," he said, "where you from?"

She answered him in patois. He, too, lapsed into it. She was almost as tall as he was.

"It is Mart'nique you living then?"

She nodded, smiling.

"You are the woman the most beautiful here," he said.

He wanted to tell her so with his hands, his thighs; with all of himself.

She smiled.

"Why I don't see you here before?"

"I don't know 'on," her voice lifting. He felt he should never let go.

"You come here often?"

"Where that, the club here?"

"Yes."

"Enough often. Everytime I coming from Mart'nique."

"And I not never see you!" It seemed impossible.

"And your man, what side he is, here or Mart'nique?"

"I don't have no man," she said, "neither here nor Mart'nique." She smiled.

"With who you come here then?"

"Eh, eh," she said, her teeth flashing, strong and even, "but with nobody. I big enough, you don't find?"

"You believe you are the woman the most beautiful in all this room?"

"Is you saying that, oui." But she was pleased.

"C'est vrai," he said.

"I want to dance with you for all the night," he said.

"But the dance nearly finish, oui." Her voice went up. Its musicality was pleasant. "You don't see it nearly finish, 'on?" The end of her statement lifted, French fashion, and hung above his head.

"I don't want nobody other to dance with you. Not now, not tomorrow. Not never."

She was laughing.

"I want to hold you as one would say you are my own."

The night was beginning again. His tiredness had dropped away from him. And his irritation and his loneliness. Here was adventure, and he could strike out like a swimmer, the entire sea before him, heading for land he knew.

Later, walking her through the pre-dawn streets, he found out she was a mother. Her small son lived with her parents in the village to the north of the island. He was five years old.

"But what age you?" he asked.

"I have twenty-two," she was smiling. "And you?"

"I have twenty-five."

"And what you doing?"

"Nothing," he said, "I drink."

"C'est tout?" She had not ceased to smile.

"Oui, c'est tout."

"Mais pou'quoi alors?" She was like an indulgent mother talking to her child. She had asked the question but her attention was elsewhere. He could not answer her question seriously. She did not really expect an answer. So, suddenly, walking through the empty streets, and drunk, he became a god. He began, out of nothing, and because he felt like doing so, to create a personality.

He said, "C'est à cause de femme moi."

It was another of the possibilities the night had opened to him. He was laughing to himself as he said, "She was the woman the most beautiful in the world, more beautiful even than you. Now she is dead. Elle mort en accouchement."

"You was love her like that?"

The laughter within him was hysterical. It flowed over him in secret. It was tinged with rancidness.

"I was love her more than any other woman," he said. Then in a sudden, cunning afterthought, he added, "She was like you; you make me remember her."

"Ah, c'est pou' ça?"

"Oui, c'est pou' ça."

She believed him. And this small outpouring of his rancidness was a relief. For some time while they walked he continued to fabricate his allegory. At the end of it, he said to himself, addressing the God he did not believe in, "You, too, must have felt exactly as I do now when you were creating Man. It was a waste of time, and although he was only an imperfect symbol of what you wished to create, you continued all the same."

They left the street and followed an uphill path, unpaved, past small, unlit houses standing under the trees on either side of the path. When they came to her own, almost at the very top of the small hill, she kicked away the stone that kept her door closed and, turning to him, said, "Ecoutez, it is nearly five. In two hours I am going to see my child. C'est pas la peine à présent. You come tomorrow night, eh? You know the place now." She was not smiling for the first time since he met her. He tried to insist.

Then, watching the dawn begin to break over the small hut that was either latrine or kitchen, he gave in. He walked down the path into the growing light. Once again, now that he was alone, the hill and his home on it seemed far away. The church bells began to peal out the Angelus and in several of the houses there were lights now. People were preparing for early Mass. Here and there on the concrete pavement beneath the verandahs of houses a figure sat up on the sugar bag that had been a bed. The early breeze was fresh and light. A woman appeared in the doorway of a house and sprinkled holy water from a bottle in front of the door before she stepped down on her way to Mass.

He was already beginning to climb, very tiredly, the hill, when the lights of the town went out.

At ten o'clock that night, lying fully clothed in her small bed, he began to wonder whether she had played a trick on him. On the unpainted wooden table at the head of the bed, a saucer contained the ends of cigarettes he had smoked and the bottle of French wine she had left for him was already half-empty. The small kerosene lamp, without a chimney, threw a thick stream of black smoke up to the low, galvanized roof.

But at eleven, when the wine was finished and she still had not come, he got up from the bed, put on his shoes, and blew out the light. He had barely finished putting back the stone behind the closed door when he heard the voices coming up the slope and saw the light of a lantern coming towards the house. Quickly he went behind the small hut. It was not a kitchen.

The darkness lightened as a group of people came into the clearing in front of the house he had just left, and stood before the door.

"C'est ici," the voice of a young woman said.

"Merci," an old man's voice.

There was a noise as someone, unfamiliar with the stone behind it, tried to open the door.

"Mais c'est fermé," the old male voice again. It was the old man who had tried to open the door.

"Non, c'est pas fermé," the young woman's voice and the noise of the stone as it moved over the earth, "c'est pierre – 'a, it's the stone."

"Bon Dieu, Bon Dieu," a new voice, a woman's and old. Then sounds on the wooden floor of the room. His cigarette butts were all inside.

"Bon Dieu, Bon Dieu." It was like the wringing of hands.

Some more movement. Then the old male voice saying, "Oui, c'est ici."

John stood in the unpleasant smell, listening. Accustomed now to the dark, his eyes could make out the low bush that began at the edge of the clearing behind the latrine. He could not pass there.

"Only yesterday all alone, she was dancing with us at the club," the young female voice.

"Bon Dieu, Bon Dieu."

"She had no luck, jamais de la chance," the old man said. "Mais Dieu save. God knows."

John heard the quick sound of footsteps running up the slope and the laughter in the voice as it sang almost, "Agnita, you come back? I have a good joke for you." It was a gay voice, young, and shouted well before the owner had come to the house. "I thought you was never coming again." There was laughter, a great deal of laughter, in the voice. The owner was already savouring the joke she was about to share with Agnita. But she must have reached the clearing for the footsteps stopped and the same voice, more reserved, went on. "Pardon," it said, "I thought it was Agnita who was come." And almost immediately after this, and with alarm now, "But what, what is arrived?"

"Agnita mort," the first young voice said.

"Mon Dieu, pas vrai," the latest voice, "Agnita mort?"

"Oui, Agnita mort."

Sobbing and the old woman's voice, "Bon Dieu, Bon Dieu."

"Mais ca qui 'rrive?" the newest voice, "what happen?"

He stood in the unpleasant smell of the dark and listened.

He had met her only once and had lusted after her. He had wished to hold her breasts, to feel her beneath him. Only this morning she had been alive.

And the old woman's broken voice, "Bon Dieu, Bon Dieu."

Her teeth flashed under the hot, brilliant lights of the dance hall.

"You believe you are the woman the most beautiful in this room?"

"Is you who saying that, oui." The final word rose musically.

"And you, what you doing?"

"Nothing. I drink."

"'Restez. Where you going at this hour. It late already, Agnita.'" The old woman's voice, "'Tomorrow you will go.' But she did not want. 'I have to go,' she saying, 'I cannot stay tonight.' And when the bus turn, is she alone that die."

"And suppose she has made a fool of me?" lying in her bed and watching the smoke from the unchimneyed lamp rise to the conical roof. "Suppose she made me come here for nothing," lying in her bed and drinking the unsweetened French wine she had placed on the table with the French cigarettes for him. "'I have to go,' she saying, 'I cannot stay tonight.'"

As quietly as he could, he moved away from the latrine while the people were inside the house, and went carefully down the stony, uneven slope of the path. When he thought they could not hear him he began to run. He walked only when he came to the paved street where the town began. The late Sunday night lay quietly, punctuated by street lamps at long intervals, and there was an air of desertion all along the empty street. He moved quickly towards the centre of the town, lighting a cigarette. The small wooden houses stood as if untenanted and around the bulbs of the street lamps insects flitted, knocked blindly, once, against the lit glass, and dropped to the ground. When he reached the town's centre, the lights in the display windows of the stores had already been put out, and the first cars were returning from the cinema.

He turned away from the oncoming crowd of people walking home from the cinema and headed for the wharf. He walked down the main street, past the closed, impersonal, business houses, past the policeman at the gate, past the barrels of fruit and the empty wooden boxes, past the tarpaulin-covered load of flour with its watchman, and walked, to its end, the thin, concrete edge of the dimly lit, empty wharf. Very softly the water lapped the piles the wharf stood upon. Away from the piles, without the light, the water was dark, and now and then he heard the sound of fish breaking its quiet surface. He sat on the iron stanchion at the end of the concrete walk and looked out over the water to the peninsula from whose top the lighthouse cast its turning beam at regular intervals. On the other peninsula he saw the lights of the hospital and below them the single light that marked where the morgue was and where the body of the girl now lay.

He smoked quietly for some time. The lights of the hospital went out one after another. Presently the whole of the outjutting was in darkness except when the lighthouse flashed its brilliant, whirling light and where, after the hill was in darkness again, only one light showed, like a point, at the water's edge.

John had once walked down the irregular path that led to the morgue and had watched the floating body of a sailor, fully clothed and head down in the water, the trousers' legs ballooning with the collected liquid, and the absurdly dangling arms and the whole floating mass of him performing an informal dance to the rhythm of the small waves. But that had been during the day, and he had not known the drowned man; and his death had not touched him. But she had come out of her own little life, whatever it had been, to meet him. And she had left her touch even more than Stephen or his mother had done. And she, a complete stranger. He smoked quietly in the dark. He would have gone to bed with that stranger. Perhaps he might have had a child with that stranger.

The light, the only one that had lit the wharf, went out suddenly, jerking him. He sat in the dark on the iron mooring of the wharf and one of his conversations with the old minister came to him. He had been reacting to Stephen's suicide and to the selfishness he believed, and would always believe, he had discovered in himself that day on the beach when he had not moved. They were drinking punch in the old man's room.

"It's a pity we should so be able to affect other people's lives," he had said.

And the old man said, "It's a law. 'No man is an island entire of himself.' It was Donne who wrote that."

"It would be better if we were. Every man would be his and his responsibility alone." He was feeling acutely the effect of the deaths of Stephen and of his mother, separately and together, and it had been intolerable that he should have to.

But the old man said, "It can't be helped. Forever I shall have affected your life. And you mine."

"It's unfair," John said afraid of how greatly his existence must have shaped and qualified his mother's. "It seems to me that neither you nor I should have that right."

"No man," the old man said, "has, or has not, the right to do anything."

Now, sitting on the wharf, he was eager to believe this. He wanted, sitting in the warm rising wind from over the sea that brushed his cheek, not to have been as affected as he was by the death of someone he had not really known. He did not want to accept that Agnita, he had not even known that her name was Agnita, any more than Stephen or his mother, should have the right to leave him marked by her death.

Then, speaking still in the context of Stephen's suicide and remembering his own immobility on the sand, he said, "Nothing seems real but selfishness." And the old man, "There's love. And for some there's religion."

"You left religion, you gave it up."

"No. I haven't left religion. But to talk about it would be too involved now. But even religion can, for some people, be good."

"It was not good for Stephen. It didn't help him."

John heard the old voice of Agnita's father, "Pas de chance. Mais Dieu save, God knows." And the lamenting voice of her mother, "Bon Dieu, Bon Dieu. Good God."

He knew now what made gods possible. And religion too. They gave the lie to reality and carried man safely across the inexplicable. They turned him into a child again, made him irresponsible, freed him from the load of himself. And of others. And sitting alone in the dark, it occurred to him that if Stephen despaired, it was because he lost confidence in his God and, losing it, was confronted with the ultimate, final authority for the first time – himself. The revelation of his God, incarnate, but made man now only in himself, might have been too much for him to bear. And his suicide, far from being an act of despair, might have been one of revolt.

Stephen had embraced religion because it promised Life after death. And yet his suicide had not been to enable him to get to that

Life after death but to escape the one before it. It was a gesture not unlike the one of somebody who refuses, with a wave of the hands, another's argument, pushing it away. Anne-Marie had thought Mr Dezauzay would be better off dead. He himself had been glad that his mother had died. And his own life, empty as it had seemed at the time, had conserved its importance for him. It had given no pleasure, afforded no satisfaction, made no promise. It had merely rolled on. He decided that his reaction to his mother's death had been as intrusive as her solicitousness about him had been. He would feel neither regret nor sorrow for the dead girl, whose wake he seemed to be keeping now. Nor any pleasure. And henceforth no death would shock him no matter how sudden nor contradictory that death had seemed.

He arose from the iron mooring just as the church clock struck the first notes of twelve. He walked uptown along the empty streets. Driven by the wind, a piece of paper passed him noisily. A cat crossed the street and disappeared into the darkness of the other side. The business houses stood shut, cold and remote. He wanted a drink and his cigarettes had run out. But it was Sunday and the town, at this hour, was a dead town. He had no desire for sleep. He dreaded the walk back to his room. He walked, therefore, the quiet streets and chose that part of the town where the small shops and the rum-shops were, half-hoping he might find one of them open. He had no luck. He walked through the lingering smell of rum and fried foods, past huddled figures bedded down for the night on their bags, past decrepit wooden houses, through the smell of stale urine, until the smell of freshly baked bread roused him and made him aware that, also, he was hungry. He walked into the yard and entered the bakery. Black men, bare-chested and sweaty, were sitting on wooden boxes among huge baskets of bread. Their aprons were grimy, and the wooden counter on which they had kneaded the bread was white with dried, caked flour. The floor was a mixture of caked flour and dirt, a colour almost like that of the faces of the men themselves; and all about there was the sharp, dry smell of fresh bread and the crackling of the cooling loaves in the baskets.

"Bonsoir," he greeted the men.

They seemed tired. They mumbled their answer and looked at

him, unmoving and with sweaty expressionless faces. He bought bread, bummed two cigarettes, for which they would not accept payment, and went out again into the night. The hot bread burnt his hands and he chewed with his mouth open to let the cool air inside it.

9

He began to read again, enormously, and at random. He slept late, read, went for walks over the hill, and played chess. He went every week to the library that faced the church from the opposite side of Columbus Square. But he had grown accustomed to his home on the hill and he refused to leave it. In any case, when his mother's house was sold and his father, he discovered, had put the money into his account, he had nowhere to go.

He spent long hours among the English dead in the small military cemetery on the hill. He glimpsed the futility of human effort. It was here, after all, that it ended always. Except for those who were able to leave of themselves behind. Stephen had wished to be one of them. His death, John thought, with the contradiction of its manner, gave the lie to his existence when it should have completed, or, at least, testified to it. The men whose graves he looked at had killed others and had come here to die. What had motivated them? No more, perhaps, than the need to eat and their subscription to the current propaganda their country fed them. Their predecessors, having killed off the original inhabitants, had fought men from other countries for his black ancestors and for the island. Their followers were to unite not once but several times with men from those same countries to fight against others. Expediency, utility and, ultimately, self-interest, national or individual, was the only criterion. He learnt to distrust group endeavour of any kind and to pay no attention to the slogans they threw ahead of them. Alone, he walked, read and thought. And, with the old man, he played chess. He was alone even on those Saturday evenings which he had resumed after some weeks following Agnita's death, drinking and talking with those he sat with.

And alone, too, and increasingly, he thought about Miriam.

As Harold plunged more deeply into the life he had returned to, John saw him infrequently only. But with his friend, the old priest, he did go to the party which, six months after he had come back, Harold threw to celebrate his birthday and the new house he had moved in to.

Harold had done well in his profession. He told John and the old man, whom he had picked up early in order that he might be at home to receive his guests, that he could not complain.

"I'm doing as well as any one of them," he said.

They were sitting, having already looked at the new house, on the verandah that went all around it. They were drinking rum and water, Harold, whisky and soda, while they waited. Anne-Marie was the first guest to arrive and the men rose to receive her. Harold took her inside and when they came back she had a double rum-and-water and Harold had to leave because the other guests were beginning to arrive. John introduced his friends, who shook hands.

"You're the young lady who came to my house one night," the old man said.

"Yes," John said, answering for Anne-Marie.

"She was looking for you, I think."

"It looks like a good party," Anne-Marie said to the old man. "Did you see the food? I'll eat and eat…"

Her expressed sensuality merely reinforced that already disengaged by her person. She gave the impression that she possessed the capacity for full, uninhibited physical enjoyment. She would eat as much as she wanted to, drink as much as she wished, and would enjoy both with the same animal satisfaction, the same eagerness, the same total immersement, as that which she would bring to her dancing later on. Or, John thought, as she had brought to her affair with Derek.

"I love parties also," the old man said, his eyes twinkling his appreciation, "especially your West Indian ones."

He, too, was eager. But his eagerness seemed tired next to Anne-Marie's. John had visions of her, elegant, sensuous and beautiful, going on forever, like a glittering top, forever spinning under the bright lights of all the drawing-rooms of the world.

Outside, the cars were following one another rapidly to the

house. The drawing-room before which they were sitting was already animated with much talk.

"I'm going for a drink," John said, "anyone?"

Anne-Marie emptied her glass. It had been nearly full.

"Another double," she said, "plenty rum, little water."

The old man still had his first drink.

"I'm taking my time if I have to last," he said. He smiled. His effeminacy was subdued, like his excitement. John went for the drinks.

When he came back, Anne-Marie and the old minister had left their seats. She had joined a group of men and waved her hand and called to him. The old minister was talking to one of the older doctors. John, not fully at ease, looked for Harold. He found him talking to a young white man with a beard. John had never seen him before.

Harold said, "Johan, this is John, friend of mine. John, Johan."

"How do you do."

"Pleased to meet you."

"What're you drinking, Johan? I see there's no need to ask John."

"Rum and water. Double."

He was not English. Harold brought the drink and said, "You serve yourself after this. You eat, when you want, as much as you can."

"Very good."

"Johan is one of our new doctors," Harold told John.

"Not new," the un-English voice said, "not after six months."

"Johan is a Pole," Harold said. "He can't speak English as we can."

It was a joke and they laughed at it. Johan spoke English more like English than John's. And he had his own language, too. Much later on, when the party was moving by itself and Harold was freer, he told John that the doctor was not a doctor at all. A Jew, he had fled to England where, after the war, he had resumed his medical studies. He had been compelled, in his fifth year, to interrupt his studies for the second time; and, hearing from West Indians in England that doctors were scarce, had come here in order to raise the money he needed to continue.

"Doing well, too," Harold said. "Smart. Accepts chickens and things like that instead of money sometimes."

Johan had, it seemed, brought with him the latest drugs and a less perfunctory examination of his clients. The people flocked to him.

John was shocked.

"How could this happen?" he wanted to know.

"Oh, there was some story of lost certificates in Poland and I vouched for him with the Government here. A thing like that isn't difficult. If you know how. He's been good to me, too, for that."

John had visions of payments made by a grateful student to his friend. But he only said, "But, Harold, the man is not a doctor."

"Doesn't matter. We need doctors anyway. Half a loaf, as they say."

He dismissed considerations of ethics with a wave of his hand.

"He's really good, too. And almost a doctor besides."

John was not sure whether Harold's conviction was his own or the result of the medical student's generosity.

"But this is a secret between us," Harold said. He moved away and began to talk to someone else.

Now, people were dancing. When they were not dancing, the men were mostly standing out on the verandah. The women sat inside. Anne-Marie was outside with the men. The old minister was talking earnestly now with a fairly aged man whose hair was very white. Mr Roderick Beaulieu, de Beaulieu, as he called himself to his close friends, was a senior civil servant, amateur painter and historian of the island. He was not interested in his work in the Service and had ceased a long time ago to be efficient. His cousins, however, were influential and his stock as historian and painter was high on the island. He was, therefore, transferred from department to department and, always, on promotion. He lived alone in a large house away from the town, his English wife, with their daughter, having long returned to England. He was soft spoken and very self-consciously assured and, for years, he had been travelling throughout the island collecting data for a book he was writing on the cultural roots and habits of its people.

"I think it's terribly important, of course, but I cannot be sure yet, naturally," John heard as he passed. The old minister, his back to John, had not seen him. John moved through the crowd on the verandah, resting, so to speak, on the fringe of each, as if for breath. As soon as his glass was empty, he went inside and filled it again.

He had been waiting for Miriam to arrive ever since Harold had said she was coming. It seemed now, so late, that she would not. He had not seen her since that evening at the club the day after the party for Harold. He was, now, absolutely delighted to see her again. She came up the steps to the verandah, unnoticed by the men who were drinking and talking on it, sought, and after some time, found Harold, and accompanied him inside where she accepted some punch. Then she lingered with him before joining one of the groups of women talking inside.

From the verandah he watched her. He had been drinking steadily throughout the night and was quite drunk. He was standing without any group, alone, and feeling the consequences of his persistent drinking. On the edge of one of the groups Johan was standing, drunk, red in the face. His glass was empty, like John's, and it seemed, like John also, that he didn't really belong to any group here. John went up and asked him to have a drink with him. They went inside. Miriam was talking to the elderly wife of one of the town's oldest lawyers. She did not see him. As he looked at her, she raised her hand to her hair. There was nothing in it. But the gesture pleased him, for some reason or other, very much indeed. John and the medical student took their drinks back with them to the verandah. The party had been going for nearly four hours, and now the first of the guests were beginning to leave. John and the student were leaning against the rail of the verandah, facing the room. The old priest joined them. He was smiling. He was ruddy even to the folds at the back of his neck from the drinking, his gestures, as he talked, multiplied, his effeminacy disengaged frankly now from all of his flabby frame, his eyes twinkling. He stood with them a moment, his wide hips bulging his coat, animated, eager, not at all a priest, speaking with his hands, his eagerness a little desperate, John thought, the oldest, the flabbiest, perhaps the happiest man at the party. Then he was gone.

Inside, Anne-Marie was swinging. Her hair had come undone and hung over her shoulders. John could not decide which of the two was enjoying the party more. John and the student spoke for a long time together. The Jew spoke of Poland, the war, of cruelty and of oppression. John spoke of the West Indies, of slavery and what a recent thing it was, about the Haitian Revolution. They had something in common: an identity to establish, a position to assert, a phantom to flesh. They were two beings in an alien world: one, traditional, recognized, persecuted; the other, young, emergent, as yet unrecognizable to itself or others. One was lost because too observed. The other because too unobserved.

Johan talked of freedom, longed for acceptance and for an end to all persecution. He was, he said, although he was a Jew, perhaps because he was a Jew, worried about the current talk in the West Indies about Nationalism. He distrusted it. The sickness, he said, would begin with John's politicians and would eat through like a cancer. It would thrive on the ignorance of the electorate, on the disinterring of what had been forgotten and were now insults. And the writers, the ones who were not careful, would speak of evolution and progress, like the politicians. It was a mess, but that was where it would end, as it always did.

Listening to the earnest, drunken student, John watched Miriam as she arose from where she had been speaking, and went out, he guessed, to look for Harold. He had not spoken to her. He watched her say goodbye to Harold, descend the steps and disappear into the night away from the area of light from the verandah. When he heard the sound of the car which was giving her a lift into town, he went inside to get more drinks for himself and for Johan.

"What we need," Johan said, "is intelligence and understanding."

He had a horror of war and had seen it from too close not to be afraid of it.

"In your time," he said, "these islands have not known it. Lucky them."

He was wrong, of course. The islands had known war but only peripherally. And so, to speak, tentatively.

They talked and drank. The party was becoming noisier now

that the elder folk had left. Inside, Anne-Marie was dancing. Her partner was making her laugh. John was very sorry now that he had not spoken to Miriam. And, as it had been in the past when he thought of Miriam, he thought now of Stephen. He wondered how Miriam would react if she found out that he had killed himself. He would never be the one to tell her. He was sure of that.

Inside, Anne-Marie and her partner, alone on the floor, were swinging wildly. It seemed they had only just begun to dance. The party was gradually coming to an end. Anne-Marie and her partner were dancing every number and were themselves select-ing the records they wanted. At one o'clock only a few of Harold's friends remained. They brought chairs on to the verandah and settled to serious drinking. After a while, Anne-Marie and her partner, whom John had not recognized but thought he knew, came also from the dance floor and joined the drinkers.

While they drank, they discussed government policy, salary revisions, the assistant administrator and the next assizes. They complained about the cost of living, the insufficiency of car allowance and were amazed that Government still paid his full salary to the chap who, after so many years, still had not qualified in England. They discussed cricket, of course, and island transfers within the Service and whether it was better to work in St. Kitts or in Grenada. What they talked about was not important. It was merely to enable them to provide a background for their drink-ing. Then the young man who had been dancing with Anne-Marie said, "Christ, Harold, let's talk about something else."

"What you want to talk about, man?" Albert asked. He was an old schoolmate, now a lawyer.

"Tell us what you want us to talk about, Dennys," Harold said.

John recognized the name and through the haze of his drunk-enness, the man also. When they were schoolboys, Dennys used to paint posters to advertise the school sports. Everybody had thought his posters were the best the school had had for a long time. He had not finished school and, some years after he left, had disappeared. He had always wished to paint, he said. It must have been more than nine years, according to John's drunken calcula-tion, since he had seen Dennys. Suddenly, unwilling to listen any more, and noticing that neither Johan nor the old minister was in the group, John got up and walked, a bit uncertainly, along the verandah to the comparative dark behind the bedrooms. On the way he stopped inside to fill his glass. Through the window which looked out on to the verandah he saw the old man asleep on Harold's bed. He did not see Johan. He supposed he had left. He sat alone at the top of the steps leading down to Harold's garage and began to smoke.

Across the flat, dark sheet of water at the foot of the hill where he sat, he looked at the lights of the town, half a mile away, and at the red pilot light that showed behind the town and guided ships away from the shallows when they were entering the harbour. Near that light Miriam lived. But the red light stood out alone from the dark that surrounded it. John felt he had been foolish not to have spoken to Miriam when he had so much wanted to do so. He saw her again talking to the elderly wife of the lawyer. At the same time, she was speaking to himself. But he could say nothing of what he wished to when he tried to speak to her. It was as if now that they were together he could find nothing to say. But she was a very real presence now in his drunken mind.

"Why are you wearing black?"

"I'm mourning for my life."

It was Derek who had first mentioned those lines to him.

"You're mourning for his life," he said aloud, "and mourning does not become Electra."

John blinked rapidly in the dark and shook his head with violence and with his mouth tightly closed as if from the effort.

"And doesn't she know it?" he asked aloud.

But it wasn't any good. The image he spoke to was a succession of images of a composite Miriam, made up of half-smile, half-broken-faced grief, of former happiness and later acceptance, of resolute and intelligent forgetting, some fixed in attitudes he had not even known he noticed at the time, following and impinging upon one another like a faulty kaleidoscope, and his words were not applicable to any single one of them.

He got up, his drink finished, and went into the bright, empty sitting-room. He poured himself a full glass of rum-and-water. He had to lean for some time against the edge of the table before he could begin again to walk out from the room. Miriam was talking to the elderly woman, and she did not see him. This time he smiled at her. Her head was bowed and she was listening respectfully to what the elderly matron was saying.

"Suicide." The word, as yet, was in his mind only and he uttered it as he might have held something he was trying to evaluate by the feel of it. Miriam looked up from her conversation, saw him, and smiled.

"Suicide." He spoke the word aloud.

This time it was not a smile she gave him. It was frankly a laugh. He laughed too. But, already, she had ceased to look at him. He staggered across to where she sat. She was no longer there. He turned to look for her. He heard the sound of the car driving her away. He sat down. He was tired. He raised his head and she was there in the doorway, laughing as he had so often seen her laugh at the more funny of Stephen's other antics. This one was the biggest of all. But she was dressed in black, too, as he had never seen her before and, while she laughed, her face was distraught with listening to him. He laughed at her, with sadness, and his face dropped to his chest. She was gone when he raised it again and he was alone in the empty room, his glass in his hand. He emptied it, making a face, and went to the table for a refill. The light hurt his eyes and he went out to the verandah to join the others. He sat on the floor, his back against a post for support. Distantly, the voice of Dennys, sitting not far away from him, sounded on his drunken ears.

"You see," John heard, "the island is not for me. It is for you," and did not see the arc of the painter's right hand including all his friends, "lawyers, doctors and engineers and civil servants. Me, I don't plead for it, I can't cure it, I don't build roads for it, I won't stand behind counters with deference to serve it. So," his hands were open palms upward, as an indication, "it will have none of me, except on its own terms. I can't accept them. So they call me lazy, drunkard; they say I have no ambition. I am a disgrace. What they mean, of course, is that they don't understand why I refuse to sell my freedom for money to buy a piece of dasheen or a breadfruit. They envy my independence. They try to pin me down. Nobody," he slapped his knee with conviction, "nobody can pin me down."

He opened his arms wide in front of him and continued, "They can humiliate me, make me a prostitute," he smiled and pointing, "but even Harold prostitutes his profession. So," he opened the palms of his hands and shrugged his shoulders. He took a long drink from his glass, wiped his mouth with the back of one of his long arms and settled back in the chair. From its comfortable depth, without any gesture to accompany his words this time, he said, "And I don't give two damns any more." But he could not, it seemed, be still for long. His hands were moving again, "I drink my rum and I praise my God. A piece of ass now and then and, afterwards, confession and a truce with God. He will understand; He always does." His arms expressed finality and assurance. Then they opened wide, palms upward, with the question, "What else can I do?" His right palm slit the air in front of him on the first "Stupid," then cut again rapidly and in quick succession, "Stupid, stupid, stupid." His hands were held out towards his listeners, accusingly, "A bunch of Philistines." He settled back in his chair and said, without heat now, "The thing is hopeless."

He sat up, reached forward, emptied his glass, and made it nearly full again from the bottle of rum on the floor next to his chair. Then he added a tiny bit of water. While he was doing so, Harold said, "Maybe it is, Dennys. Then if so the only thing is to compromise. Get a job and paint in your spare time."

Dennys did not answer until he had taken a deep pull on his new drink. He said, "Ah," smacked his lips, wiped his mouth and his moustache with the back of an arm and settled back in his chair. Everybody waited.

"Why don't you get a job and practise law in your spare time, Harold?" he asked softly.

"Harold's qualified," someone said, "it's his profession."

"You see?" the painter asked. "What's the use?" He shook his head, "You don't understand."

"You can get a job as a draughtsman," Albert said.

"Have you ever asked me to paint anything for you, Albert?"

"I don't need to, I have no pretensions."

"There you are," he was vindicated. At least, his gestures indicated that he felt he was. "You heard?" he asked the others. "And he's educated. What do you expect?"

"You're one of those for whom I'm lazy, aren't you, Albert?"

"I haven't detected any significant predilection for work, Dennys."

"Oh, what's the use?" the painter cried, slapping his knee with exasperation, "what's the bloody use? You others, you don't understand. You go away and come back qualified, like millions of others all over the world. You come back here. And all you think of is money, money, money," his hands were chopping out the words from the air in front of him, "and your place in the island's warm social sun, mass-produced in your education, mass-produced in your intentions afterwards; empty, empty, empty."

His snobbery, his artistic arrogance vis-a-vis the professionalism of most of those he spoke to, his artist's egotism, real or born only of his frustration, had reached its high point. He emptied his glass and filled it again.

"You're all a bunch of fakes," Dennys said. His disdain might have been drunken: it was no less real for being so.

"Why don't you go away then?" someone asked.

"Because I'm lazy. I'm broke and I don't care any more. Trapped. That's what." His hands embraced his imaginary self in the trap they formed.

John raised his head. The words of the painter alarmed him. But he could not hold it up. It sagged again upon his chest.

"I'm beaten by this island, beaten by the ignorance of the people, by the obtuseness of its professional elite, seduced by the fact that, no matter what happens to me here, I'll never die of starvation. I'm drunk most of the time anyhow."

"You're a coward," Albert said, "you don't even have the courage of your own convictions."

"My dear Albert," the painter said, "I'm as obstinate in my profession as you in yours. And just as courageous too." Albert was supposed not to be very successful in his profession. Nevertheless he possessed a car and he could afford to be condescending and superior to his drunk and completely unsuccessful friend. He smiled.

"Your envy is showing," he said.

"Envy?" the painter was genuinely surprised. "Why should I

118

envy you when we are in the same boat? Both of us are trapped, Albert, both of us. We are not doing what we should, you and I. I because the island does not, perhaps cannot, permit me to yet, and you, because you made a foolish choice. You chose law for what you could get out of it. And now you're trapped in it."

Anne-Marie, sitting beside the drunken Dennys and listening as she drank, was attracted. His stubbornness, his refusal to conform even while he seemed headed for certain social disaster, fascinated her. She admired his mad, unthinking independence and, already heady from the rum and the dancing, basked in the metaphorical warmth of his closeness to her. It was possible the painter exaggerated: his talent, his attitude no less than his speech and the gestures that accompanied them. Her intelligence told her so. But the kinship she felt for him now was not based on the intelligence. And, in any case, she had been mentally nodding her head in agreement with much of what he had been saying. The discordance between his pessimism and his obvious physical vitality, not unlike Derek's, was like something strange she would like to dwell upon. And he was handsome too. In the battle against the Alberts and the Harolds, she was on his side, directed, in going there, by her own earlier, totally unpleasant contact with the values she thought they represented. His intensity, the single-mindedness of his passion, seemed to elicit a vibration of those very qualities in her. And she experienced a feeling of joy that was at once the result of the too much drink, the elation after the dancing, and the discovery of this spirit in so many ways kindred to hers.

Yet she had to admit that this was not all. There was in her decision, when she was mentally taking sides, some of her former dislike for Harold. It was true that a lot of the arrogance and the sharpness of the tongue she had recoiled from in the early days seemed to have remained in England. But the ambition, obviously, was still there. And the efficiency in fulfilling it. Harold's father, Mr Montague, had not attended the party. The rumours she had had of a complete break of the never strong relationship between father and son must be true. And Harold, undoubtedly, was a success. Anne-Marie was not sure his father would have cared much for that success. It was Mr Montague himself who had said to her, "My boy is angry with me. That makes him cruel with everybody." He had been waiting for her to come down from the apartment and he was standing in the door of his grocery with a gift for her in his hand. He spoke patois. "Don't mind him," he said and wiped away her tears. "Perhaps later, when he have what he want, he will be kind again. And he will get what he want. I know that."

That evening when Derek visited her and she told him what Harold had said to her, speaking of their relationship, he had only laughed.

"He's only saying it," Derek said, "he doesn't really mean it."

His good-naturedness had surprised, though it had not consoled her.

"Harold wasn't talking to you alone," he said.

Mr Montague had been right. Harold had got what he wanted. At least was beginning to get what he wanted. But the tales about him were rampant. He had already acquired, after only six months, quite a few small estates as well as the disdain, and the envy, of many of his colleagues. A good lawyer, he had achieved results that had been sometimes as startling as they had been unexpected. He never turned away a client and he never failed to collect all of his fees. And there hung about him more than a faint smell of dishonesty and the unattractive aura of opportunism and exploitation.

Anne-Marie, looking at Harold, smiled at him. They were friends. Almost. She defended him against her friends' suggestions that he was homosexual. He had not married, did not seem interested in any of the women who looked at him. And he must have known what was being said about him. But he did not care. Their opinion did not matter now.

He had other things. His ambition, his practice, his drinking and his sports. He still played, and well, football, cricket and tennis.

And even now that he was not sober, he still continued, she reflected, to be elegant.

"How are the politics coming, Harold?" she asked maliciously.

His passage into politics was another stage in that journey he had mapped out for himself towards ultimate, absolute self-fulfilment. And he had begun by writing articles in the island's newspaper that were adverse to government. He disdained to use a pseudonym.

"Oh," he said, "coming on."

But he turned away from her and from the topic and continued to speak to the man next to him. He did not wish to discuss it.

Next to her, Dennys was talking now, not very coherently, to Johan who had emerged from somewhere within the house. John seemed asleep. She got up and went inside for more ice. When she came back she poured herself a long rum-and-water. In one hand she held a piece of chicken she had taken from the table inside. The night wore on. The party's rearguard finally broke up. But she and the painter ended the night, or rather, the morning, dancing, drinking and talking in one of the night clubs on the edge of the sea.

10

Anne-Marie was not asleep. On her back, through the changing red and black behind her closed eyelids, she sensed the movement in the sun of the tree under which she lay. She opened her eyes, turning over, and propped herself on her elbows with an effort. She had tried to sleep. But, insistently, the image of her schoolhood, surprised earlier between the pages of a book, had continued to stare at her. She turned over on her back, her hands under her head, and closed her eyes once more. The interchange of red and black behind the eyelids would, but for the memory, have been soothing.

She did not remember when the faded photograph had been taken. But she knew, from the uniform she wore, that it must have been before the day when, leaving school at twelve, she had walked through the streets to her home, her ears ringing still from the information they had received that had not been meant for her, feeling examined by myriad eyes from behind closed shutters and hearing in her mind the malicious whisperings of people who had always known, had never once been fooled, had always been listening from behind the barricade of their knowledge, to the steady stream of their silent, mocking laughter.

She remembered little of that contained flight through the streets. What she remembered was the shock of opening the heavy, wooden door of her father's house and being confronted with the carpeted staircase that rose behind it, solidly, familiarly, its cleanliness almost antiseptic, and of the gloom behind the closed door after the sun, and the feeling, once so secure, as of entering the quiet dark of the church. Leaning against the spotless walls of the corridor she had retched, watching her vomit seep through the thick carpet, its edge slowly widening and discolouring the expensive material as it spread. Then, relieved, she climbed up the stairs and entered the drawing-room. The thick, wide carpet that covered the wooden floor over her father's store and that muffled her footsteps was spotless. The cushions, in their black and gold covers and the island's beauty reproduced in golden thread upon them, were beaten into perfect shape as though they were not meant to be sat upon. The straight-backed, black-enamelled, wooden chairs stood as if they were mourning in the solemnity of their ordered appearance. And, in the corner, her father's rocking chair rested, tall, dominating the rest of the furniture, waiting to resume, after the day's business hours, the gentle movement that her father had been imparting to it for years now. She had walked, feeling an alien in that familiar room, under the gaze of her ancestors, her father's family, and stood at the door of the smaller room where her father was waiting for her to join him for lunch. Today she did not walk across to join him where he sat. And she did not kiss him on the cheek before they began to eat.

Watching him, she noticed for the first time how the thin line of his body, in the baggy envelope of his white drill suit which slanted sharply down at the shoulders, seemed to be against the very centre of the straight back of the chair. On either side of it the old, polished mahogany formed an equidistant background. She felt that the polished mahogany table between them, on curved legs and set for two, diffusing the smell of day-old roses from the glass vase on its very centre, was at once a barrier and a protection.

D'aubain looked at the beauty of his daughter's face, the long beribboned braids of her black hair, her elegance in the elegant school uniform she wore. But he said nothing and turned his eyes away. It was this that saved Anne-Marie's resolve. If he had continued to stare at her she might not have had the courage to continue the onslaught on their established habits that, by not kissing him, she had initiated. Even as she was sensing this her father turned again to look at her. But the aristocratic calm he might have inherited from his French ancestors who had survived the Terror could not subdue her now. She was roused again. And in a rush, without her seeming to have any control over them, her words asked the question she had come to ask.

D'aubain seemed not to have heard.

"Is it true?" Anne-Marie asked.

It was as if, in an effort to keep herself in reserve for later, she was being deliberately curt now.

D'aubain did not answer. His composure and his steady stare agitated her more.

She could not be surprised at her boldness when she spoke again. She was not aware of it.

"Tell me," she stamped her foot. It made not the slightest sound on the deep, soft carpet.

Still he stared.

"Tell me, tell me. Why are you afraid to speak?"

In her agitation she raised her voice. It must have surprised her father very much. Yet, looking at him, it seemed he had not noticed any irregularity in their domestic life.

"You are afraid. You are. You are."

He was afraid.

He was afraid, and therefore it must be true. It was true. There was no longer any doubt. There had never really been any.

"You lied to me. You who so often spoke against lying. You lied to me."

He spoke now, still calm.

"I did it for your sake."

"You lied. You deceived me. You. A hypocrite!"

If she had expected him to flinch she would have been disappointed. But she had not. She was too agitated to try to provoke him by what she said. It came out naturally pushed by her exasperation and her disgust.

Suddenly, weakened by the violence of her still largely pent-up emotion, and possessor now of the truth, she felt she could stand no longer. She stepped into the room and, drawing one of the chairs away from the table, sat on it.

"All this is sham and pretence," she said, holding the front of her expensive school uniform, "sham and pretence." It was as if she would have liked to tear it away from contact with her skin. "I shall wear it no longer."

"I did it for you," D'aubain repeated, murmuring. The lips, in the near-white face, seemed hardly to move.

"You knew. Your friends. Perhaps their children too. I only…"

"No, no," he said, beginning at last to be agitated himself, the flow of his words covering that of hers so that their talking was like two streams flowing together, the muddy water of the one mingling with, and yet flowing parallel to the clear, unsullied water of the other. "My friends would never…"

"They all knew except me."

He shook his head.

"Everybody. Everybody knew. Why didn't you tell me?"

He could not find anything to say. Perhaps he had many things to say and did not know how to say them. For she was crying now. And it distressed him.

"False, false," she murmured between her sobs. "Why did you? How could you? You. You who spoke so often to me about honesty and about truth."

"I did it for you. To spare you."

She looked at him. It was as if she had a revelation.

"No," she said, "you did it for yourself."

"Anne-Marie!"

His surprise was genuine, histrionic as his unusual outburst might have seemed. He had never had any doubt when he had taken his decision long ago, that all he was doing was for her. If he had contacted the Mother Superior of the convent to arrange for Anne-Marie not to wear the cheap school uniform that would symbolize her illegitimacy for herself and for the rest of the town, he had done so, not for himself, but out of his love for her. He had not questioned the system of double uniforms. He had sought merely to circumvent the inconvenience to himself and to his child. D'aubain, behind the mask of his face, composed once more, was surprised by this thought he had not looked at before. To his child and to himself, that was what the thought had said. To himself. He shook his head mentally. No. It had not been for himself. He had had nothing at all to gain. Whatever he had done could only have been for her. So many of his friends and cousins had illegitimate children and they had not bothered to go to the trouble he had gone to. He had had very definitely the feeling that he was protecting his daughter. To protect her had been the only consideration. He was no reformer, social or otherwise. He had wanted to spare his daughter. Not fight a crusade. To spare his daughter, not himself. "Il faut les éduquer d'une manière très pratique, monsieur," was what the French nun had said. She had no doubts about the system. It was perfectly clear that the system was just, that "le peuple", that was the word she consistently used, had to be taught in a very practical way the disadvantages of "loose, animal union". And when she added, "Et vous, monsieur, vous auriez dû le savoir," the prick of her censure before she agreed to his request had seemed worth submitting to. He had, first and foremost, indeed, only, been concerned with his daughter. Not with himself. Nor any principle.

He had never stopped to think that his successful attempt to prevent his daughter from being marked was in itself an indictment. And the dishonesty of his procedure with the nun had been as unapparent as if it had in fact never been. He was not exactly one of "le peuple". The irony of his existence on the island and of the existence of an entire class of people like him, dying out to be sure, but owing to the very fact of the illegitimacy of his French forebears, was lost upon him. He had not thought of those things at the time. He had had his daughter only in mind.

He had not wished for her. At thirty, unmarried, and under the very strict sense of conventional propriety that, as yet leaders of the town in all matters, his society, forgetting its origins, had learnt to acquire, he had found it increasingly comfortable to conduct quiet and very proper sexual relationships with his servants. And Anne-Marie's mother had neither been the first nor the last of these. He had not questioned his unmarried state. He had not particularly wished an heir either. Or an heiress. Yet, when Stephanie told him she was pregnant, he had not altogether been displeased. When the child was born, on one of his cousins' estates, Stephanie was sent to Barbados where she had been living ever since. So long as she did not come back to the island she would continue to receive money, letters and photographs of her daughter.

D'aubain looked at the weeping girl, so beautiful, he thought. He himself was so ugly. The consequences of his premature birth had been a source of ridicule to no one more than it had been to Cazaubon, his father. The handsome man had perhaps felt it necessary to vent his disappointment in his only child in the form of jokes to his friends, cloaking it with the cynical veil of his laughter as if, by being the first to laugh, he might thwart those others who wished to do so. His insistence on his son's full participation in the social life around him might have been for his son's sake. It might also have been the result of a perverse need to show his fortitude before this disaster in his personal life by exposing it in public and making fun of it there. As soon as he could, that is, as soon as his father had died, D'aubain ceased to take any part in the social life of his group. His rocking chair, in large measure, and his solitary walks at night, had made up for it.

D'aubain looked at his daughter. She was beautiful and he could discern traces in her face of his own mother. It was Cazaubon's love for his wife that had directed his rancour and his disappointment upon his infirm son. That love had, in its completeness, eliminated all possibility of blame for the deformed offspring she gave him and for her barrenness afterwards. It was as if his deformed son had desecrated the beautiful woman, his wife, who had had to bear him. As if that son, in making claims upon his love, could only turn it into hate. When Cazaubon died, D'aubain felt as if a strong rope that had held him had snapped. Alone (his mother, whom he had so much loved and had not dared to show his love to in his father's presence, had died years before), he had to look for something that was solid enough to replace, not in exactly the same way, but with the same suggestion of control, his father's attitude. He felt the need for some anchor, something he could hold on to; something to offset the anarchy of his features and of the life it had placed before him.

His sense of order had been the result of that search. Order and stability in all spheres of his existence. And when Anne-Marie was born a miracle seemed to have been performed. The beauty of his daughter when he saw her for the first time, the traces of his dead mother and of Stephanie's handsomeness, the incipient regularity of the not yet fully-formed face, everything about her seemed at once a justification of that sense of order and proportion he had learnt to appreciate, a tangible expression of his attainment of it, and a huge personal joy and satisfaction. Nothing, he had vowed then, nothing that was irregular in any way, would touch this orderly and well-formed result of his own irregularity.

Grown now, she was talking even as he reflected. The indictment of his motives rolled off her lips but he heard now only a small part of what she was saying so imperfectly because of her tears. Yet, even in the small part that he heard, the accusations hurt him profoundly. He would, he decided, more than a little afraid, not even try to answer them.

He got up from his chair and walked to the open window behind it. In the yard Millicienne was watering the flowers. He watched her, his back to the tirade of his daughter's words, as if he would thus shut them off. In the yard the flowers stood row upon colourful row. He was about to send Millicienne away. He changed his mind and sighed mentally. It probably would be of no use to do so. He stood at the window and watched her and listened to his daughter. He was relieved when she left the room. He returned to the table then and had lunch alone. He did not enjoy it, did not feel like eating it. He ate slowly, completely upset, and, as completely, controlling it.

Anne-Marie had rushed off to her room. She tore her uniform away from her body. Its feel on her skin was abhorrent. Its elegance was at once symbol of her father's duplicity and the hypocrisy of an entire existence. She threw herself on the bed and, almost immediately, for her emotion had tired her, fell asleep. She did not go to school the next day, nor the day after it. She did not see her father either on those two days. But the disintegration of the fabric of their personal relationship was the prelude to the greater disintegration, more gradual, of the entire fabric of her previous existence. Out of this disintegration, like plants sprouting from decomposing weeds that had grown on the very spot, her new life developed and expanded, achieving a new diversity, social and moral, that overran the former plot lines of its exclusiveness.

For her father she still continued the habit of meals in common. It was the only one she preserved.

11

Her meeting with Derek had been one of the results of her new existence. Anne-Marie opened her eyes, turned herself again on to her elbows and, looking across the glare, saw him. There he was sitting on the sand, bulking out of his swim suit, playing with one of his sons. As she watched his handsome blackness she was feeling acutely the pain of her reminiscence and of his presence, already equivocal and, besides, so curiously tied up with her relationship with Dennys, with her own feeling for Derek, and with the friendship that linked them all together. It was as if she were divided; the part that was Dennys' looking down detachedly at the other part which would always, in essence, belong to Derek, and would always feel the pain of the past. The split in her was not new. Only different. Her schizophrenia, after Derek's letter, had been the only thing to save her and to enable her to move under the watchful eyes of those who seemed not to be watching, with a composure that had required all of her will to maintain. Now they were watching again.

She saw that Derek had ceased to play with his son and was looking at her. She waved at him. He smiled and returned the wave. His smile and the wave that accompanied it were so familiar to her. I'm playing a game, she thought, looking at him across the glare and at herself looking at him and at everybody looking at them together. She wondered whether he, too, felt he was playing a game and how much he felt manipulated, wound up and set down like a toy. This reserve was not natural. Or was it, now that they were adults? She would have liked to be free with Derek. It would have meant nothing at all. She belonged now to Dennys. At least the part that was his, Derek could not take away; and the part which was Derek's, Dennys had not tried to take away. Their spheres were exclusive. And she wanted to enjoy both equally. It was her privilege, surely. She had earned it. Or, having once earned it, had she lost it now to Sheila? The figure of the white girl still thin and sickly-looking, stood out like a pillar, centrally, in the foreground of the picture in her mind. And yet for her, Anne-Marie felt nothing, neither dislike, sympathy nor even any form of jealousy. There was Dennys; and their relationship was perfectly clear. And there was Derek; and their relationship was, too, perfectly clear. She was happy now with Dennys. She had been happy with Derek. What she wanted was the right to savour that happiness, not actually, she did not wish to, but like someone looking on the photograph of the place where, once, he had had a very enjoyable holiday. Or like the person returning to walk along the same beach but with his suit instead of his trunks and his pleasure, in his memory, intensified by the feel and the sight of that which had once evoked it. Derek was there and she, too, was there.

Anne-Marie smiled and turned away towards the sea. Derek was playing with his son again. The waves rolled in boisterously from the Atlantic and the sun on the water hurt her eyes. She was not happy. But she was not unhappy either. Happiness or unhappiness were words only now. She closed her eyes. Grains of sand carried by the wind knocked against the lids as she lowered her chin on her folded arms. She felt tired, as after a long swim. Her tiredness was not unpleasant nor unrefreshed. The feeling was like sinking, all breath exhaled, slowly in the warm water. One sometimes felt one should like to sink so pleasantly forever. Then there was the pain in the chest, the need for air and the quick push back to the surface. Always there was the need to be reasonable. Or else.

She sighed. She had so rarely been. And she had been so happy once, not being. Happy. Happy? Yes, she had been. There was no doubt about it. But she had also been happy while she so successfully hid her private desolation from those who watched her. And the shock her relationship with Derek had provoked had pleased her enormously. One didn't question happiness, though, nor look at it too closely. The wind was blowing sand against her face and into her ears. The waves broke. The trees moved in the wind.

Had she been happy? Or had she merely played at being happy? And if she had been, in what had her happiness consisted? How much of it had been because, refusing to be manipulated, she had perceived an intense emotion in performing actions that would, normally, have given merely pleasure. To love was not rare nor, the popular films notwithstanding, even wonderful. But to love when love was prohibited, to walk when they expected you to fall, to laugh when they waited for you to cry, then that was something else.

But now she no longer had anything to fool them about.

She must always, she supposed, be grateful to Derek for writing to tell her, long enough before, that he was going to marry this English girl. When the news reached the island she had already encased herself. And when friends asked, "I hear Derek is married, is it true?" she had been able to answer, with no trace of anything in her voice, that it was true.

She lay again on her back, her eyes open, and watched the play of the coconut leaves against the sky and the clouds that moved beneath it. She liked to think that Derek's decision to practise in England, the war notwithstanding, had been, partly, because of her. He had always been thoughtful and considerate. It had been his consideration, even before the arrival of his letter, that had made her anxious. It had come after a period of non-writing irreconcilable with the Derek she had known. Her unanswered letter had given more cause for worry. Fear and a growing awareness of fragility had combined then to form something she had striven to chide herself for and which she called lack of faith. And when the letter came, its softness, its tactfulness, its consideration, had not been able to dull the edges of its thrust. She had feared, been uncertain, suspected; and she had been chiding herself for doing so. The letter, with its information, the end that it brought to her doubts and the unbearable sensation of suspicion and hope, had avoided any defence she might have constructed, anticipating, during the period of silence that had preceded it. He had made a white girl pregnant and was going to marry her.

131

She could not have been surprised that Derek had made anyone pregnant. She and Derek had made love on the beach during the day and the night, they had made love in the sea, and they had made love at night behind the closed, heavy door of the corridor in her father's house. For months after he had left, her body, which he had awakened and sensitized, tingled with the desire to make love to him. When Derek left she had suddenly found herself alone. When his final letter came, the loneliness, which had already been mitigated, while she waited, by the certainty of her expectation, was re-found. "To know," she had written to him, "is better than not to know." Well she knew. Knew also that the end had come. Well, she thought now, an end, not the end.

But she had only been able to make the grammatical distinction later, much later, when, at Harold's party, she had seen Dennys, almost with his belly up, on the stream of his disillusion and unhappiness.

Anne-Marie turned again and rested on her elbows, her eyes open. Sheila had joined Derek now. The children were on the sand beside them. The rest of the party, too, having slept, were emerging from under the coconuts. She waited for a while and, since she did not see him come out, went to look for Dennys.

She found him under the sea grape, a nearly-empty quart of rum at his side.

"Aha," he said, "caught at last."

He was very drunk. He sat up, patted the ground next to him, and motioned her to sit down.

"Will you come into my parlour?" he asked as she sat down next to him.

She did not speak. Already, he was touching her everywhere at once. Anne-Marie sat, her eyes closed. Behind her eyelids it was dark only now for the sun could not penetrate the tops of the sea grape under which they sat.

"My little whore," he said, "my precious, gratifying, inexpendable whore."

His hands were between her swimsuit and her skin.

She said, "Darling, you drink too much."

"And if I don't," he misquoted, "why chaos is come again."

She smiled. She did not insist. Her statement had been no censure. It mattered nothing at all to her whether he was drunk or sober. She watched him, waiting, while he played with her. The touch of his hands stimulated her. She sat and waited. He lay back on the sand, his head on her lap, face downwards, sniffing.

"Ah," he said, and breathed deeply, "ah, ah, ah." He raised his head slightly then dropped it, making noises without any meaning as if he would bore a hole through her lap with his burrowing face. She sat, patting his head, waiting.

"Smells good," he said.

She smiled unseen. He had been kissing the bathsuit under his face. He bit suddenly.

"Oh," she said, "that hurt." But he didn't do it again. Her fingers were in his hair. He sat up and drank the last of the rum. Then he looked at her.

"Want some more?" she asked, translating the question asked by his raised eyebrows into her words. He handed the empty bottle to her. She took it and stood up to get the new bottle. He threw himself at her feet and tripped her.

"Oh," was all she said. But it gave her much pleasure. She hoped it gave him pleasure too.

"Don't you want the rum?" she asked, for his hands were all over her fallen body.

Whatever he wanted she would give him, when he wanted it and where. He took his hands away.

When she came back with the bottle, he was asleep on the sand.

12

Dennys awoke with an intense pain in his chest. He realized he must be in hospital and, still drunk, resumed, in his mind, his driving Derek's new car, Anne-Marie's sudden scream, the instinctive swerve to the right, and, in the fraction of the second before the impact, the body of the stationary lorry leaping out at him from behind the sharp turn of the road. It occurred to him that Anne-Marie must have died.

"Nurse."

"Nurse," he called out again.

The nurse came.

"She's dead, isn't she?" he said.

She shook her head. But she was young and still in training, and only incompletely professional. Her hesitancy betrayed her. And when he said, "Oh God," she did not contradict him.

As soon as she went out of the ward, Dennys came down from the bed, put his weight on his left leg, and fell down. But he got up again and, watched by the other patients, at once scared of his reputation for rowdiness and disapproving of his action, hobbled out on to the back verandah. He followed it to the stairs leading to the back of the hospital, descended, went past the Resident's bungalow, and followed painfully the track that led downhill to the mortuary at the sea's edge. He went inside. He had to stand for a few seconds to allow his eyes to become accustomed to the half-light within the small room. The body on the slab was that of a man. He came outside again. He would have to go to the town. He could not follow the road because they would stop him and take him back to the hospital. Without a word and only after a very slight hesitation, he began to walk along the water's edge towards the town. Soon he came to where the sea pushed itself stagnantly between the short rocky promontory he had just clambered over and a similar one on its farther side. He began to wade across, the water, in places, reaching up to his knees.

"I am sorry," the Vicar General said, "but I can do nothing. The church does not waver on this point. You know that," he turned to Derek. He had to raise his voice for the sound of the drumming and of the flutes, which had been approaching all the time, came up very loudly from the street just outside the presbytery. It was so close that it could not cover the other noise of the shuffling feet of the masqueraders and of the several children who followed them.

"We cannot give her a burial, you understand?" he said in his French-inflected English. Years of living on the island had not improved it. "I cannot even believe Miss D'aubain would have wished for it."

Outside, the feverish rolling of the drumming and the shrill, gnomish musicality of the flutes had increased. The noise sounded just outside of the presbytery. The Vicar General smiled and rose from his seat. "I am very sorry," he said, "but there is nothing I can do." Derek took the hand that he offered but Harold was already at the door, his back to the Frenchman, and seemed unaware that the priest had offered him his hand. Outside the masqueraders were performing in front of the presbytery and young priests were taking pictures of them from the verandah. The priests were throwing coins down to the street.

"We'd better see the carpenter now," Harold said. He was deliberately keeping his anger in check. The car started, waited for the dancers to get to the side of the street, and moved quickly away from the curb. The noise of the drumming and the sound of the bamboo flutes receded but, as they turned a corner, was resumed again. Everywhere, bands of masqueraders were celebrating the anniversary of the discovery of the island by Columbus, the Genoese.

Harold and Derek commissioned the coffin from the carpenter, engaged a hearse, and found a woman to wash the body. Then they telephoned the hospital to find out if Dennys had regained consciousness. They were told that he had and that he had also disappeared from the hospital. They got into the car and followed the road that led, past the river and along one side of the harbour, to the hospital, slowly, looking for Dennys. They did not see him.

Dennys was tired. He had been making his way slowly over rocks and through water for over an hour. His chest and his left knee hurt him. The cigarettes in his trousers pockets were wet. He wanted a drink. He sat on the rocky outjutting and, looking at the depth of the water that lay between him and further progress towards the town, he despaired. He knew he was not strong enough now to swim across it. And the hill rose too steeply for him, with his injured knee, to scramble over it. He lay face upwards on the rocky surface and shut his eyes against the sun, the pain and his anguish.

Harold and Derek left the hospital and drove back to the house where Anne-Marie was being washed. They went past the group of curious people, gathered outside and making their comments in patois to one another, and entered the drawing-room. Miriam was in the room where the body was, with Sheila. John was smoking in the kitchen. The noise of drumming and flute music seemed to come from all the points of the town at once. The result in the quiet room, except when one of the bands was very close, was an inharmonious agglomeration of sound, conflicting, muted with distance, but pervasive, and as grotesque as a musical parody. Derek announced the news of Dennys' escape from the hospital. Nobody could imagine where he could have gone to. Not one of them believed he might have been trying to get to the town by following the line of the edge of the sea. The only thing, they decided, was to wait. Harold drove Sheila and Miriam to their homes. Derek told John what the Vicar General had said. John asked why they couldn't just take Anne-Marie's body to the cemetery.

"It would be too much scandal," Derek said.

"It's scandal already. This could hardly be a matter of degree."

"Everybody would talk about it."

"They'll talk anyhow," John said. "You know Anne-Marie wouldn't mind."

"They'd talk about nothing else for years."

"So what? Let them."

And as if to control his anger he took out a cigarette and began to smoke.

"Jesus Christ," he said.

"Maybe we could take her to the church and say a prayer ourselves," Derek suggested.

"How will that help Anne-Marie, Derek?"

"I don't know."

"Or, for that matter, how would it help, to pay those priests to hold a funeral?"

"Everybody's buried," Derek said, "everybody wants a funeral."

"You mean everybody alive wants a funeral for the dead? And the priests more than anyone else."

"It serves no purpose getting annoyed."

"Those bastards have no right to come here and do that."

"You may be annoyed," Derek said, "but that's no reason to be silly. The problem of Anne-Marie remains with us."

"Anne-Marie's no problem, Derek."

"Now she is," Derek said.

"The bastards," John said again. "They don't even take the trouble to learn to speak English properly. They know it doesn't matter what they preach. Nobody listens anyway."

He had sat through how many sermons while priests newly arrived from France tried out their English. The sermons had been unintelligible. Now they dared to refuse to bury Anne-Marie. Once walking past the church he had watched the Vicar General chasing the men and women who were standing on the pavement in front of it. He had treated them like children.

"The bastards," he said again. And he remembered, then, long-forgotten Sunday afternoons on the beach with the other boys and Father Galet. But he had been only one.

Harold came in.

"Albert telephoned," he said. "Wanted to know what time was the funeral. I said I'd let him know later. Says his car is down and he wants to come with Lafond. He supposed Lafond would be playing the organ. I didn't say anything."

Lafond was Anne-Marie's boss, the island's Accountant General, and Albert's neighbour. He had succeeded old Dezauzay and was chief organist at the cathedral.

"We haven't decided what to do yet," Derek said.

"There's nothing to decide," Harold said. He was still annoyed with the Vicar General. "We've got to bury her, that's all."

"No church?" Derek asked.

"You Catholics," Harold expostulated.

Then after a pause he asked, "Would you mind if she were given a funeral by my church?"

"The Methodist? No."

"A waste of time," John said. "We can take her to the cemetery. If you must pray you can pray there."

"I agree with John," Harold said, "but if you like I can talk to Weekes."

Weekes was the Barbados-born Methodist minister.

"I don't know that there's anything in it," Harold said, "but there's no harm in trying though."

They drove off in Harold's car to the rectory.

The Reverend Weekes was unwilling. "I don't see how I can do anything now," he told them, speaking to Harold. Reverend Weekes was a black, gentle, little man. He had only recently come to the island and was unwilling to do anything that might be polemical or could bring about conflict. He had been particularly warned against this on an island which was virtually a Roman Catholic stronghold. He did not say so, however. He merely decided that, when he saw Harold again alone, he would explain more fully to him. The friends left the rectory and went back to the car.

"What do we do now?" John asked.

Harold and himself were looking at Derek.

"We take her to church ourselves," Derek said. "Then we take her to the cemetery."

The others agreed.

"How about four o'clock?" Derek suggested.

"That's about the usual time," John said.

"Make it quite clear to all that it's irregular," John said, bitterly, "you don't want to offend people nor to make enemies."

"Yes, we'd better let them know that it will not be a real funeral.

Then those who wish not to be associated may stay away." Derek's was a statement about desired procedure only. There was no bitterness.

"I wouldn't have told a soul," Harold said.

They began to plan.

"But first," Derek said, "shall we try once more to find Dennys?"

They drove up again to the hospital. They did not see Dennys. But at one point they passed a crowd of children that was much larger than any of those that followed the masqueraders, skipping and shouting, clapping their hands. They were following Old Alphonse released, not so long ago, from the lunatic asylum. Harold had to stop the car to allow the wave of gleeful children to pass.

"Roll up the windows," he said.

They rolled the windows up. They waited almost five minutes for the last of the children to pass. Old Alphonse, dressed in somebody's discarded black suit, bore a huge signboard, specially prepared for the occasion, upon which his refrain was painted in large irregular red letters. The old shoemaker was smiling, still comparatively sober, and the procession that he led was as much tradition on the island as the masqueraders whose followers his own so greatly outnumbered. Derek laughed. Harold said something about putting Alphonse back into the lunatic asylum.

Alone in the back of the car John remembered the Sunday Alphonse had passed while he had been talking to Miriam at her home. He had spoken to her only three times since that day and the third time had been yesterday, on the beach, before the news had arrived that Anne-Marie had died in a car accident. And, just as the first time, that Sunday, Alphonse had evoked Stephen for him, so now, he evoked Miriam as he had seen her on the beach standing against the coconut tree only yesterday.

"Roll down the glass," Harold said, "it's getting hot in here."

He had to reverse and turn into another street.

Dennys thought he must have been lying there for over two hours. His chest and his knee hurt. The rock under him was very, very hot. He got up. He could hardly bear to look over the water for the glare. He scrambled to the lowest rocky ledge and, on his belly, immersed his head in the water. The water was hot. He was hungry, obsessed by a desire for drink. He closed his eyes and shook his head as violently as the pain in his chest would allow him to. It was as if he wanted to transmit his anguish on the slight wind that was blowing to someone else, to anyone more capable of bearing it. He sat down again. A canoe appeared from behind the bend of the rocky outthrust and he could scarcely believe his eyes. He called and waved. And the fishermen, surprised, rowed up to the rocky ledge upon which Dennys stood, moving past the bamboo float from which the fishpot they had come to raise hung down into the water.

"The funeral is at four," Albert told Mr Lafond who was having lunch with his sister.

"Thanks, Albert," he stammered. "But… er… what class? First or Second?" He stammered a great deal and took a long time to say anything. Albert waited patiently while he spoke. "I didn't hear any bells, so couldn't know if it was a First Class Funeral or a Second. I know Miss D'aubain would not want to have a Third Class Funeral. Maybe I should phone the priest."

"The church has refused to bury her," Albert said. It would have taken the same time for Mr Lafond to say less than half of the sentence Albert had uttered.

"But," stammered Mr Lafond, disturbed and, therefore, taking even longer to utter his sentence, "you said the funeral was at four."

"I should have said we're going to the church at four. There'll not be any priest."

"Oh," Mr Lafond said very, very quickly. "I see." It sounded like one word.

He looked towards his sister who was sitting at the table eating and listening to the conversation.

Miss Lafond, for she too was unmarried, said, "Then you mustn't go, James. The Vicar General will not like it."

"Anne-Marie, I mean Miss D'aubain, worked in Mr Lafond's office," Albert said.

"He mustn't go. Don't go, James," she said. "A man in your position cannot attend things like that."

"Well, he can lend me his car then. I have a breakdown."

"No, no, no, no," very quickly, "I'll take you. I promised," turning to his sister. He had worked his way through the Service and at fifty-one had acquired a healthy respect for property, especially his own.

Millicent Lafond said, "Drop him in town, James, and come back. But don't go to that thing."

"That's all right, Millie," he said over a long time, "I know what I'll do."

"Well, all right." She was piqued. "Excuse me," she said to Albert and went inside.

Stammering much Mr Lafond promised that he would take Albert as he had promised into the town in time for the funeral at four o'clock.

Albert was laughing as he returned to his house.

Dennys got out of the canoe, nearly fell, and walked up the small pebbly beach behind which the huts of the fishermen stood. The piece of roasted breadfruit he had eaten had lessened his hunger, but he was still very thirsty. He sat and waited while the men pulled their canoe up the slope of beach and, since they had refused the dollar he had offered them, went with them to the small rum-shop. It was full of fishermen and their women. He called for a pint of white rum for the men who had rescued him and a can of beer, first, for himself, unmindful of the questions and the explanations that were going on all about him in patois. He drank the beer and, refreshed, shared the white rum with the two men and one or two friends who had joined them. When the rum was finished he thanked them again and bought a quarter bottle of Martiniquan rum which, out of politeness, they refused to partake of. He gave them half a pint of white rum which they accepted. He went out again. The wide, ungrassed space at the back of the huts, normally filled with playing children, was empty. The smell of filth from the two canals that bordered it rose with the heat and mingled with the smell of stale fish and rotting wood. He walked along one of the canals past the big tree the fishermen generally mended their nets under. There was nobody there. Distantly from the town the sound of drumming and flute music came to him. A woman, a table on her head, passed him going to the town. Behind her a man walked carrying a huge basket from which the top of an ice-cream freezer showed. Dennys looked at the sun and guessed it was already long past two o'clock. To get to Anne-Marie's house he would have to walk the length of the town to its far side. He doubted he could do so. It would be easier to sit on the concrete steps near the Botanical Gardens and wait for the funeral. He crossed the pitched road leading to the town and entered the Gardens. The drumming and the sound of the bamboo flutes came from the town, seemingly quite close sometimes, and, at others, becoming almost inaudible as the wind dropped. He wanted to get to the stone steps quickly. He was afraid he might miss the procession. But he was tired, and his injuries hurt, and he could only make his way slowly.

Anne-Marie, washed, dressed in white, lay in the drawing-room, her hands crossed over her abdomen. To keep the flies away from her bruised, powdered face, an old woman, her servant, was brushing the air over it with a white kerchief. On chairs set against the walls people were sitting, speaking in low tones against the ever-changing volume of flute and drum. In the kitchen, John and Derek were drinking with the carpenter and the driver of the hearse. Because of the heat they had removed their jackets and were standing in their shirt-sleeves in the too-small kitchen. Even so they were perspiring much.

"As soon as Harold comes we start," Derek said, "O.K.?"

"I wonder where Dennys is?" John said.

Earlier, Harold and Derek had gone to the painter's home. They found it locked. Nobody they questioned had either seen or heard anything of the painter. A car stopped now outside behind the hearse. Harold and another man, the accountant in the Treasury where Anne-Marie had worked, came in through the back door which was near to the kitchen.

"Four o'clock," Harold said.

He went into the drawing-room. The accountant accepted a drink in the kitchen. The carpenter had followed Harold into the drawing-room. He came back now, the lid of the coffin having been screwed down. But there was no room for him and he had

142

to stand in the door. It was very hot. Derek and John, their coats back on, Harold and the driver of the hearse took the coffin outside and rolled it into the back of the hearse. The driver got into his seat. The funeral began to move slowly, as the horse, feeling the pull of the reins, headed for the church. Standing in the doorway of the house, the old servant, the white kerchief now on her face, watched them go. The noise of the drumming and the flutes seemed still to come from everywhere at once.

The procession stopped in front of the church. The town square next to the church was covered with flags and bunting. From tables laden with children's merchandise children were buying noisily. Other children were in lorries waiting to go on joyrides through the town, for which they paid a penny, or were noisily returning from them. The noise they made was mingled with the cries of the hawkers and the noises of children playing on the lawns. And above all this, the sound of drumming reverberated, received and sent back, amplified several times over, by the vaulty, hollow church.

"The bells," Dennys thought, "I've heard no bells."

He had been sitting on the stone steps for some time before he realized that he had not heard the church bells. He was very tired now. Neither the pain in his chest nor the one in his left knee had improved.

"There's no funeral," he thought. "Nobody's dead."

He raised his head as if to look through his bemused senses with concentration at this new thought.

"Nobody's dead. Anne-Marie isn't dead. Anne-Marie's alive."

The excitement of his drunken hope made him quiver. He got up and went down the rest of the steps to the road.

"Alive."

"She was not dead."

"She was alive."

He was moving down the road, in the sun again, towards the town. His head swirled and eddied with the thought of Anne-Marie's existence.

"Alive."

"She was alive."

If he could, he would have run all the way to the town.

But he could only walk very painfully now. In the unexpectedness of his hope, in the confusion of his tired, drunken mind, Anne-Marie was resumed as the sensation itself of her existence. It was her essence, the idea of her alive, not her image, that moved like a mad wind around the corners of his brain. He thought he was moving quickly over the empty road. He was still too far from the town to meet the dancers but the sound of the drumming and of the flutes was becoming increasingly louder. Then a lorry passed filled with children who shouted and laughed at him. Soon another went by and he heard his name and the derisive laughter of the merry children. He walked on. The sun was on his head and his mad thoughts were swirling within it. It was as if his head was on fire now. He was almost on the outskirts of the town. He heard in the distance the swelling roar of a huge crowd of children shouting something that he did not understand. The roar swelled and advanced as he walked. The wave of sound was advancing rapidly. Already it had engulfed the other one of the drums, dominating it with the reverberating outbursts of its own expression on the town's empty edge.

Then he knew. The words, MARY MUST COME BACK, arose above the other miscellaneous noises. It was Old Alphonse. The size of the crowd, when he saw it, astonished him. He had no time to move out of its way. He was surrounded by deliriously happy children who pushed and jostled him, their black faces shining with sweat, their teeth showing as they cried, skipping and jumping in a huge mass that not only filled the entire street but spread out as well to the very edges of the small wooden houses that stood behind the pavements on either side. The noise of their shouting deafened him. He tried to get out. He was pushed inevitably back into the centre of the crowd. Almost beside him the black-robed figure of Alphonse, completely drunk, seemed less to be moving on its own accord than driven forward, as he himself was being driven forward, by the mad mass of shrieking children.

Quickly tired he allowed himself to be carried on his feet. He was like a ship afloat on a sea of bobbing black heads. He raised his own. He saw, emerging from behind the corner of the street a block and a half away, and advancing towards the sea of children, the horse first, then the hearse, and behind it, Harold's car.

His panic emptied him like a pricked balloon. The sea of black heads bore him forward and the rest of the funeral procession appeared slowly from behind the corner ahead of him. He watched it. The shouts and cries of the children around him continued. But, ahead, the first of the crowd had seen the procession, come to a halt on the left side of the street, and were beginning to slow the mad pace of their advance and to half-smother the fierceness of their cries. Against their relative immobility the rest of the surging crowd hurled itself, was compacted, moved forward a little, then came back, slowly, as from a slightly rubberized wall. The pressure on his body increased. Cries of discomfort arose around him. He heard the words "Horse" and "Funeral" more clearly as the tumult of shouting began to subside. Close to him, Old Alphonse, his lower body wedged tight by the compression of black children, was swaying, his head on his chest, prevented from falling only by the mass that bore him. For an instant the mob of children was still. Then as the leaders began again to reorganize their movement, undecided whether to go past the stalled funeral procession or turn on their tracks, it seethed again into movement that was confused and without progression. It no longer chanted the refrain. It heaved and moved, progresslessly, with the milling activity of worms in a pit latrine. Slowly and with difficulty he was able to inch his way forward. Near the hearse the confusion was the greatest. The children were afraid of the horse which was becoming restive. They were being slowly pushed nearer to it, trying to resist, and moving away from it and from the nearness of the dead body it carried. They flowed onto the pavement to the left of the hearse and onto the street on its right leaving a fairly wide space around it.

Dennys emerged finally into that open space and, for a moment, stood alone in the sun. Then he walked towards the hearse. The children began to look at him. Derek, Harold and John got out of their car and went to him. Derek took his hand and said, "Let's get into the car." Dennys shook his head. They stood in the open space for some time. The three friends were trying to get

145

Dennys to get into the car with them. He refused. On the side of the streets the children were reorganizing and watching. The shouting was dying down. The milling too. The horse was becoming calmer. Dennys walked away from his friends and went to the back of the hearse. Behind their leaders the children were moving now to the side of the street and to the pavements behind them. The street was almost clear. Alphonse, his feet in the gutter, sat on the edge of the pavement on the side of the street away from the hearse.

Dennys opened the glass doors at the back of the hearse and sat next to the coffin, his feet dangling. The driver had come down from his seat in the front and was talking to him. The children were watching. Dennys was beginning to gesticulate now as he spoke. The children, who had not been able to hear anything that the grown-ups had said before, heard Dennys plainly now. Derek took the driver aside and spoke to him. The children did not hear what he said. The driver left Derek, shaking his head, and went back to his seat. Dennys still sat at the back of the hearse, his feet dangling over the edge. The glass windows were open on either side of him. Sometimes one moved and the sun was reflected in little dazzles of light from the moving glass. Derek walked from where he had called the driver to speak to him and went over to his two friends who were standing in front of Dennys and talking to him in low tones. The three friends went back to Harold's car. The procession began to move again along the street through the lane of children who were standing at its sides. Dennys sat at the back of the hearse. He had removed the unfinished quarter bottle of rum from his pocket and was drinking from it. The children had never seen anyone drink rum at a procession before. They watched him. One or two began to follow the procession as it moved slowly, keeping pace with it as they walked along the sides of the road and along the pavements. Some more followed them. Then more and more. Finally all the children followed. The procession moved away from the town leaving the sound of the drumming and flute music, which had never ceased, slowly behind them. On the edge of the pavement, alone, his head on his chest, his feet in the gutter, Old Alphonse sat on his shadow in the sun.

When they came to the gate of the Botanical Gardens, out of the sound now of the flute and drumming, the procession stopped. A few cars were waiting. They contained those people who had not dared to go to the church and take part in the unauthorized funeral but who, to ease their consciences, perhaps, or to give some meaning to their protestations of friendship for the dead girl when she was alive, would accompany her now, and safely, to the cemetery. Mr Lafond, her former boss and the church organist, was one of them.

The cars sped up the climbing road between the Gardens and the sanctified bamboo glade to the cemetery. The hearse began to move, slowly at first, then with increasing speed. The children who had held back on the edge of the Gardens followed it. They were shouting and pointing at Dennys now that the ordered solemnity of the funeral procession had been disrupted by the cars.

They skipped merrily uphill behind the hearse whose speed Dennys, by his presence, and the open doors controlled. Finally the driver of the hearse decided to increase the speed. He did so and the children shrieked their pleasure as they ran up the hill behind the now trotting horse amused that Dennys had to hold on to the hearse. The coffin jolted up and down but not enough to leave the sunken area on which it lay. The pace of the hearse quickened. The smaller children fell back and sent their shouts even more loudly ahead of them. The glass doors of the hearse opened and closed repeatedly on the knees of the painter's dangling legs. His left knee was afire with pain. By the time they had got to the top of the hill, the foremost of the children were already some yards behind and still dropping back.

It was at a resumed funeral pace that the hearse continued its journey downhill to join the rest of the vehicles that waited in the sandy cemetery near the sea.

13

There had been no question of the group's holding a party for Derek similar to the one they had held for Harold when he arrived. They could not take that privilege away from Mrs Charles, his mother and their friend. On the evening of the day he arrived, therefore, the four of them, Anne-Marie, Miriam, Harold and John, went, together with Dennys, to the party which the widow had organized for her son, his wife and their children. They went early and brought gifts with them. Mrs Charles was surprised but pleased at the gifts. She did not pretend that John and the others should not have put themselves to the trouble of bringing gifts. She accepted the gifts as she had accepted the small pension they had paid her after her husband had fallen from the cable ship on which he worked and disappeared in the Atlantic. Like the pension, the gifts suggested, tacitly, that she needed help. The suggestion was less true now but to refuse the gifts or expostulate with the bearers, no matter how perfunctorily, would have been pride. And Mrs Charles was not a proud woman. She accepted them, therefore, with the same thanks, but not silent this time, as when she had accepted from Derek who just won the scholarship, the money he had saved for his study abroad. Her brown face crinkled now as she teased John and Anne-Marie, whom she had best known, for having neglected her while Derek was away. She was fatter than John remembered her; but then she had stopped taking in washing for five years and now had very little work to do. She was very happy and tried not to show it. She was proud about her son and sought to hide it. She would not have advised marriage to the white girl, a stranger but her daughter now and, therefore, a stranger no more. But she pretended that it did not matter in any way. Hers was to love her daughter white or black, and be loyal to her children, for her son's sake. Already she was making plans for the restoring of her health to the fragile and thin girl. She was sorry for Anne-Marie. But she was careful not to let her feelings show. She covered it with teasing and light banter and tried not to look too often in her direction. Her party was small. It consisted mostly of her own friends, a few of Derek's, the closest ones, and representatives of those families, including that of the administrator, she had once done washing for.

Nevertheless, John and the others held their own party for Derek and his family. It was a beach party, held more than a month after he had arrived, and planned to last from Saturday which was the usual half-working-day holiday, through Sunday, to Monday, the anniversary of the island's discovery by Columbus, and a Public Holiday. But on Sunday, late, Dennys had an accident with Derek's new car and, in it, Anne-Marie had died.

Soon after the beach party, the old minister, John's friend and companion for many months on the hill, left the island to take up an appointment to teach in one of the secondary schools in Barbados. A great part of his time had been taken up in playing chess with his friend. Now that he was gone, John found himself more alone than he had ever been. And only very infrequently now did the group, or what was now left of the group, have any occasion to get together. One day, on his way to the library, he heard that Old Archie had gone mad. He remembered the self-assured master that Archie had been. He remembered Archie's elegant handwriting on the blackboard, his bullying authority in the classroom, his departure to France and the priesthood. Then his return, broken in body and spirit, no priest; his inability to get his old job at St. Mary's College which was now held by a qualified Barbadian; his clerkship in the Civil Service at the lowest point of the salary scale. He had begun then more than ever to drink and to be transferred from department to department in the Service. In his mind John followed the older man's steady deterioration with a mesmerized attentiveness and was terrified. It was as if the path he had been tracing again in his mind for the mad, former teacher was the very one he was doomed to follow. The old, slouched figure that seemed to want to efface itself as it walked was not that of Archie but of himself. The shabby, prematurely old man, who called his former pupils, now in the Service, "Mister" and asked, too respectfully, about office routine, was not Archie but John Lestrade in ten years. The drunkard who could not drink with his contemporaries and who was too old to drink with those he did drink with and who laughed at him was John Lestrade, dead alive, suffocated by the poisonous air of the island he had not been able to get away from.

Suddenly he became confused and frightened. He began to look around him. And he began to think. His money, the money he had saved to go abroad to study, was diminishing. The time was coming when he would have to work again. He dreaded the thought. Once more he began to think of going away. Where to he did not know. What to do he did not know either. But he was beginning to feel that he had absolutely to go away. His position was worse than it had ever been. He was older, disillusioned, no longer enthusiastic. More than ever he felt like a piece of wood on that wide sea. He still read and played chess, from a book now. But there was nobody to talk to. On Saturdays he went on his round of the clubs. He drank a lot, danced a lot, talked and listened a lot. It was ordinary club talk. And it was uninteresting. He slept with women whenever he could which was almost every time he went to the clubs. But nothing preoccupied him. He was restless and afraid. And hounded by his fear even while he sought to drown it.

If only he could believe!

Believe.

He had been feeling this lack for some time now. To believe. In anything. And he thought how lucky priests were. And soldiers, too. And all those who had only to obey and take orders. All who relinquished responsibility and, relinquishing it, could never be afraid.

To believe. In anything. Even in those things he had come to discredit after Stephen had died. He could not. Nor would he believe in any God who had treated his mother as her God had done. The wheel of his life had come full circle. He had resumed his somnambulistic existence: only there was nothing at the end of it he waited to awake to. He wished he could lose himself in something. Anything, provided it was big enough or intense enough to occupy him so fully that he would not have time to look at it.

He thought sometimes of Rose and the letters they had written to each other. He remembered his impatient confidence for his life in the future. And he thought sometimes, whimsically, of himself and Rose sitting together in a bungalow similar to the one they had sat in under the windblown salt from the sea.

And he thought, with sadness and regret, of Miriam.

If only he had been able to find something to throw himself into. Something to match the completeness of Dennys' sorrow when Anne-Marie had died.

There had once been a time when he could move easily from day to unthinking day, from breakfast to school to play to study to eat to study to sleep. A rat in a trap had once been an event. A knock on the ungloved finger, by a cricket ball, or on the unpadded shin as much as the bringing down with the stone of the yellow mango. As much as the laughter of Thalia ringing in his ears while he tried to get out of the mud where the pigs were and into which he had fallen, chasing her.

Where was the relevance and the meaning now?

And why could he not now perform his actions as he had performed them then?

Innocence?

Or was it ignorance?

Ignorance.

Then was it folly to know?

To know. To know what?

He had learnt that all his actions were consolatory only, a veil between him and his existence; and he could no longer perform them without being aware that each one was a trick.

Were tricks then necessary to life?

To be a child again. That had been Stephen's wish when, walking one day, they had seen children playing on the lawns of Columbus Square.

Stephen's wish was not much different from his now. For the faith he believed he needed, he could only acquire if he were a boy again throwing stones at mangoes, playing cricket on the beach, understanding nothing but doing everything, his head down and with assurance, because tomorrow was as sure as yesterday had been, so sure, that one never bothered to think about it.

So sure, that death was a calamity.

He could never again believe this.

And he was confused.

And frightened.

One day at the bank he was pleasantly surprised to meet again a cashier he knew and who had been away for four years working in banks in Jamaica, St. Kitts, and Trinidad. For a brief month, while they had been preparing for their final examination at school, they had been thrown together. Later on she had spoken to him of plans to go away and do a degree. He found out now that she was happy and content in her job. She was about to be married. He had nothing to say to her. He left. He felt insecure and directionless. And very much alone. He was envious of her adaptability and of what he called the linear development of her life.

He had to go away.

More of those who had been at school with him and been away were returning now. One or two who had gone to become priests had returned, not frocked, and were leading normal lives with their wives or their mistresses. They walked the streets like everybody else. It was difficult for him not to smile when he realized that, between what they were doing now, and having to walk the streets with white or black gowns and get the adulating approbation of an entire town, there had been very little indeed. Ill health, perhaps, reaction to the European climate or, as it is so often stated, a lack of real vocation. These had not succeeded in escaping and they had come back. They worked now as clerks in the stores or in the Service.

They were "failures".

One or two, like Harold, were successful and happy in their success.

Many had come back from the oil refineries in Aruba and Curacao with money, the vernacular of those islands, a Latin-American twist to their dress and their dancing and, among the more intelligent and ambitious, an intention of paying their way through universities in Canada or England.

He envied Dennys' conviction and his beaten acceptance.

He envied the seemingly quiet complacency of the returned clerks, the finance of those who had come from the refineries.

He longed for the independence that Harold and the other professionals represented.

One day he attended Mass at which his friend, now Father Thomas, was officiating. The cathedral was full as it is only on the single Mass on Good Friday. And afterwards, when he was out of earshot of the adulatory clamour of the people, walking alone up the hill to his home, he envied Father Thomas for his belief and for his assurance in it.

He walked slowly up the hill, on the road without any shadow except his own. It was at his feet and showed very firmly against the noonday light. He was alone. The old minister had gone. Dennys was in the hospital. Harold and Derek he saw less and less. Anne-Marie and Stephen were dead. As for Miriam...

Three days before the beach party for Derek he had accompanied Anne-Marie and Dennys to La Colombe, the islet off the north coast, where Dennys had hoped to finish the portrait of Anne-Marie that he had begun. On the second afternoon, after painting for several hours, Dennys said he was tired and was going for a swim. He had swum out and out and John, standing on the small beach next to Anne-Marie, had listened to her shouts to Dennys even when Dennys was no longer able to hear them.

Finally Anne-Marie said, "I wish he'd drown."

She turned away and headed for the house. He waited on the beach for Dennys who spent a long time in the water. On their way to the house they met Anne-Marie sitting on some rocks a little removed from the beach. Her face was bathed with tears.

"Why are you crying?" Dennys asked her.

"My toe," she said, not looking at him, "I hit it against a stone."

"Is it burst?"

"No. I don't think so." She still did not look up. "But it hurts, Dennys."

Dennys lifted her.

"Let me carry you," he said.

And then, walking with her in his arms, he said, "You must be more careful."

Suddenly Anne-Marie had begun to laugh. She laughed until the tears, which had stopped, began again to run down her face.

"What's the matter now?" Dennys asked.

"Nothing," she was still laughing.

"What are you laughing like that for?"

She said, "Darling, I'm laughing at you and at myself. I did not stump my toe at all."

He sucked his teeth and put her down. She was laughing as if she would never stop. John and Dennys walked away.

But that evening, when they had supped and were sitting together over drinks, she looked at him suddenly and, with quiet seriousness, said, "Darling, promise you'll never frighten me like that again. Not ever."

Dennys laughed.

She insisted, serious.

"Promise."

He would not, laughing still.

"Promise," she said, "promise me, Dennys."

She was very serious. He promised. Anne-Marie sighed and sat back again. They continued to drink.

John had not forgotten the incident. The violence to Anne-Marie of her wish on the beach seemed to differ only in its expression from the violence of his secret anger with his mother after Chou Macaque had left them. Or from the furtiveness when Mrs Dezauzay looked at her husband.

The old minister had said, "There's love too." And out of that love John had learnt there was protection. His desire to take care of Miriam and protect her had grown out of a feeling no different from his feeling of admiration and, later, pity, for his mother. And it had been perhaps, an acceptance that this might have been so that had made him speak to her during the beach party for Derek and his family.

But he would never forget how she had stood, her hand over her ears and her forehead resting against the trunk of the coconut tree. When, finally, she raised her head and looked at him, she had seemed so lost and bewildered that he would have liked to support her. But he had been afraid.

She had not fallen. She looked at him. It seemed she was looking at him from the very depths of her surprise. He felt sorry for her. She seemed about to cry.

She did not.

She said, "I've never been more surprised in all my life, John."

He said, "I thought you might have noticed…"

She was shaking her head even before he had finished speaking, slowly, with wonder, as if she were not responsible for the movement and was surprised at it.

"No, John," she said, "how could I?"

"You know now." He was unable to say what was frightening him.

"I'm sorry." It seemed she could not possibly stand much longer. Very soon she must collapse beneath the weight she seemed to be carrying of her surprise and her wonder.

He did not stop however.

"Why?" he asked.

"I don't know." It was almost a whisper; but she still had not fallen. "I only know it's impossible."

"Is it Stephen?" he asked as if he were driven. There still seemed a straw to clutch at.

She shook her head again.

"What then?" A straw, a wisp of hair, the shadow even of a straw cast on the water seemed worth struggling to hold on to.

"I don't know. Don't ask me, John. Please." She turned. She was going away. The shadow of a straw was even thinner than it had been. Or was it of hope, faint, delible, already as if it had never been? She began to move. He watched her back and the thought came suddenly that he might tell her the truth about Stephen.

In the fraction of the second that it had come and gone it had brought and left behind all the reasons why he might do so. It might turn her against Stephen. It could hurt her and she deserved it. It would surprise her and he could either stand and laugh at her discomfiture or he could hold her. In that small part of time he held her, and laughed at her, won her and lost her.

He heard himself say, "If it is for Stephen, you're wasting your time. Stephen left you. He gave you up. He committed suicide."

She looked at him, half-turned and without any sound, as if seeing him for the first time. The surprise of her discovery was obvious. And it gave him pleasure as well as hope.

Then she said: "I know, John. I have known for a long time."

It was his turn to be surprised. And to see for himself what she had been so surprised to discover.

But she was continuing to speak. It was extraordinary that he should be able to hear what she was saying.

"Anne-Marie told me. Harold told her and she told me."

But, in a sense, he had been lucky. For no sooner had she turned her back, finally, on him than the news arrived that Dennys had had an accident and Anne-Marie had died.

ABOUT THE AUTHOR

Garth St. Omer was born in Castries, St. Lucia in 1931. During the earlier 1950s St. Omer was part of a group of artists in St. Lucia including Roderick and Derek Walcott and the artist Dunstan St. Omer. In 1956 Garth St. Omer studied French and Spanish at UWI in Jamaica. During the 1960s he travelled widely, including years spent teaching in Ghana. His first publication, the novella, *Syrop*, appeared in 1964, followed by *A Room on the Hill* (1968), *Shades of Grey* (1968), *Nor Any Country* (1969) and *J-, Black Bam and the Masqueraders* in 1972. In the 1970s he moved to the USA, where he completed a doctoral thesis at Princeton University in 1975. Until his retirement as Emeritus Professor, he taught at the University of Santa Barbara in California.

CARIBBEAN MODERN CLASSICS

Now in print:

Wayne Brown, *On The Coast*
ISBN 9781845231507, pp. 115, £8.99
Introduction: Mervyn Morris

George Campbell, *First Poems*
ISBN: 9781845231491, pp.177, £.9.99
Introduction: Kwame Dawes

Jan Carew, *Black Midas*
ISBN 9781845230951, pp.272 £8.99
Introduction: Kwame Dawes

Jan Carew, *The Wild Coast*
ISBN 9781845231101, pp. 240; £8.99
Introduction: Jeremy Poynting

Austin Clarke, *Amongst Thistles and Thorns*
ISBN 9781845231477, pp.208; £8.99
Introduction: Aaron Kamugisha

Austin Clarke, *Survivors of the Crossing*
Introduction: Aaron Kamugisha
ISBN 9781845231668, pp. 208; £9.99

Neville Dawes, *The Last Enchantment*
ISBN 9781845231170, pp. 332; £9.99
Introduction: Kwame Dawes

Wilson Harris, *Heartland*
ISBN 9781845230968, pp. 104; £7.99
Introduction: Michael Mitchell

Wilson Harris, *The Eye of the Scarecrow*
ISBN 9781845231644, pp. 118, £7.99
Introduction: Michael Mitchell

George Lamming, *Of Age and Innocence*
ISBN 9781845231453, pp. 436, £14.99
Introduction: Jeremy Poynting

Earl Lovelace, *While Gods Are Falling*
ISBN 9781845231484, pp. 258; £10.99
Introduction: J. Dillon Brown

Una Marson, *Selected Poems*
ISBN 9781845231682, pp. 184; £9.99
Introduction: Alison Donnell

Edgar Mittelholzer, *Corentyne Thunder*
ISBN 9781845231118, pp. 242; £8.99
Introduction: Juanita Cox

Edgar Mittelholzer, *A Morning at the Office*
ISBN 9781845230661, pp.210; £9.99
Introduction: Raymond Ramcharitar

Edgar Mittelholzer, *Shadows Move Among Them*
ISBN 9781845230913, pp. 358; £12.99
Introduction: Rupert Roopnaraine

Edgar Mittelholzer, *The Life and Death of Sylvia*
ISBN 9781845231200, pp. 366; £12.99
Introduction: Juanita Cox

Elma Napier, *A Flying Fish Whispered*
ISBN: 9781845231026; pp. 248; July 2010; £9.99
Introduction: Evelyn O'Callaghan

Orlando Patterson, *The Children of Sisyphus*
ISBN: 9781845231026; pp. 220; January 2012; £9.99
Introduction: Kwame Dawes

Andrew Salkey, *Escape to an Autumn Pavement*
ISBN 9781845230982, pp. 220; £8.99
Introduction: Thomas Glave

Andrew Salkey, *Hurricane*
ISBN 9781845231804, pp. 101, £6.99

Andrew Salkey, *Earthquake*
ISBN 9781845231828, pp. 103, £6.99

Andrew Salkey, *Drought*
ISBN 9781845231835, pp. 121, £6.99

Andrew Salkey, *Riot*
ISBN 9781845231811, pp. 174, £7.99

Denis Williams, *Other Leopards*
ISBN 9781845230678, pp. 216; £8.99
Introduction: Victor Ramraj

Denis Williams, *The Third Temptation*
ISBN 9781845231163, pp. 108; £8.99
Introduction: Victor Ramraj

Imminent:

Roger Mais, *The Hills Were Joyful Together*

V.S. Reid, *New Day*

Orlando Patterson, *An Absence of Ruins*

Titles thereafter include...

O.R. Dathorne, *The Scholar Man*
O.R. Dathorne, *Dumplings in the Soup*
Neville Dawes, *Interim*
Wilson Harris, *The Sleepers of Roraima*
Wilson Harris, *Tumatumari*
Wilson Harris, *Ascent to Omai*
Wilson Harris, *The Age of the Rainmakers*
Marion Patrick Jones, *Panbeat*
Marion Patrick Jones, *Jouvert Morning*
George Lamming, *Water With Berries*
Roger Mais, *Black Lightning*
Edgar Mittelholzer, *Children of Kaywana*
Edgar Mittelholzer, *The Harrowing of Hubertus*
Edgar Mittelholzer, *Kaywana Blood*
Edgar Mittelholzer, *My Bones and My Flute*
Edgar Mittelholzer, *A Swarthy Boy*
Orlando Patterson, *An Absence of Ruins*
V.S. Reid, *The Leopard* (North America only)
Garth St. Omer, *Shades of Grey*
Andrew Salkey, *The Late Emancipation of Jerry Stover*
and more...

All Peepal Tree titles are available from the website
www.peepaltreepress.com
with a money back guarantee, secure credit card ordering
and fast delivery throughout the world at cost or less.

Peepal Tree Press is the home of challenging and inspiring literature
from the Caribbean and Black Britain. Visit www.peepaltreepress.com
to read sample poems and reviews, discover new authors, established
names and access a wealth of information.

Contact us at:
Peepal Tree Press, 17 King's Avenue, Leeds LS6 1QS, UK
Tel: +44 (0) 113 2451703 E-mail: contact@peepaltreepress.com